THE BONE MOTHER

CZP
ChiZine Publications

FIRST EDITION

Distributed in Canada by
Fitzhenry & Whiteside Limited
195 Allstate Parkway
Markham, Ontario L3R 4T8
Telephone: 905-477-9700
E-mail: bookinfo@fitzhenry.ca

Distributed in the U.S. by
Consortium Book Sales & Distribution
34 Thirteenth Avenue, NE, Suite 101
Minneapolis, MN 55413
Phone: (612) 746-2600
e-mail: sales.orders@cbsd.com

Library and Archives Cataloguing Data

Demchuk, David, author

The bone mother / David Demchuk.

Issued in print and electronic formats.

ISBN 978-1-77148-421-3 (softcover).--ISBN 978-1-77148-422-0 (PDF)

I. Title.

PS8557.E4663B66 2017 C813'.54 C2016-907562-1
C2016-907563-X

CHIZINE PUBLICATIONS

Peterborough, Canada
www.chizinepub.com
info@chizinepub.com

Edited by Samantha Beiko
Proofread by Leigh Teetzel

Canada Council for the Arts Conseil des arts du Canada

We acknowledge the support of the Canada Council for the Arts which last year invested $20.1 million in writing and publishing throughout Canada.

ONTARIO ARTS COUNCIL
CONSEIL DES ARTS DE L'ONTARIO
an Ontario government agency
un organisme du gouvernement de l'Ontario

Published with the generous assistance of the Ontario Arts Council.

Printed in Canada

THE BONE MOTHER

DAVID DEMCHUK

This is dedicated to my parents and grandparents, who faced horrors in war, poverty, prejudice and loss, and embraced life anew at every turn. I owe everything to them.

Maia

A Lady lives in the mirror in my p
she visits at night and calls my nam
to wake me up. She is my
Friend and Tells me stories. I
can't Tell mommy and daddy or s
will go away. She shows me he
doll and says I can play
with them. She shows me her
dresses and says I can we
Them. Her house is big with lo
of rooms. I can sleep in a ne
room every night. She has liv
in the mirror for a long
Time. She is lonely and sad.
She watched me befor I
was a baby. If I live with
her I can watch mommy
and daddy and never grow
old. She says it's easy for m
to live with her. It won't hurt
and she will come to get m
I don't mind if it hurts a
little. I am new here and dont
have any Friends. She is my
friend and I Love her.

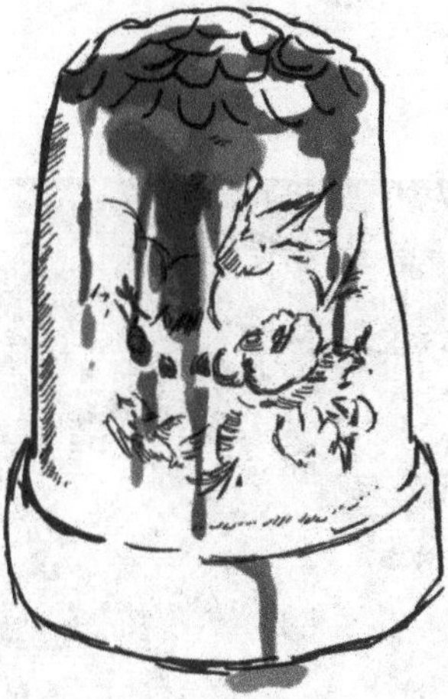

ONE
THE THIMBLE FACTORY

BORYS

My brother Sergyi and I were married in a small ceremony in our village church. Such things were possible then that now are not. This was in the years before the war, during the *movchanya*, what some call the silence, or the blight. We were farmers, our families too poor for us to be considered by the very few women our age. And we were good companions, and had been intimate since we were children. And so our bond was blessed.

Shortly after, we received the notice, and Sergyi left our farm to work at the thimble factory, as our father had when we were very small. Seventeen months later, Sergyi fell ill from pneumonia and died. The car from the factory arrived to take us to the funeral, but Mother refused to go. She instead asked that we hold a remembrance in town. The factory could not deny us this, but of course would not provide the body. He would be buried in the small graveyard just outside the factory gates. No matter. We held our own memorial. Our mother sat with me at the service, an arm's length from where Sergyi and I had stood before the priest.

She reached over and squeezed my hand. "You may

pass slowly through a valley dark and drenched with tears, but you must not rest there," she said. "These things happen."

Within two days, I received word from the thimble factory that I was to come and fulfill Sergyi's five-year contract, which had three years and seven months remaining. This dismayed my mother, who would be left to tend our farm with her aged sister, whose entire being had curled into the shape of a claw. But it was an inevitability. My mother pleaded with me to stay with the farm, and offered to send herself in my place. This would not be accepted, as we both knew. The work was difficult and arduous, and unsuited to an elderly woman. I offered to send her money to hire a hand but she refused. She would have no other men on the farm but me.

We sat and ate our supper, a pale broth of cabbage and potato with scattered shreds of mutton drifting through it. I feared the meal would be our last together. The next morning, letter in one hand, a pasteboard valise in the other, I hired a driver to take me out into the countryside and up to the factory gate.

While the Grazyn Porcelain Factory also produced fine china for homes, hotels, and restaurants, near and far, it was celebrated the world over—as we in the village were frequently told—for the exquisite porcelain thimbles that had been manufactured for centuries using closely-guarded techniques developed by the Grazyn family. Every *tsaritsa* since Anastasia Romanovna had received a priceless Grazyn thimble as part of her wedding trousseau. The factory produced only three hundred and thirty thimbles a year, each painstakingly formed from a special paste, then glazed and fired by hand. The workers lived there, ate there, slept there, for the duration of their contracts, and were then sent home with lifelong pensions—enough to clothe and house and feed their now-estranged families.

I recalled as I rang the bell that I had known many such workers over the years, but that none had ever spoken of their time there. Even our father was silent on the matter, and we learned early on not to raise the subject.

After a moment, the door opened, and I was ushered inside. My belongings were taken from me, and I was led to a locker room where I was handed a pair of grey overalls, a fine-fitting pair of lambskin gloves, a kerchief for my hair and a cotton mask for my face. I changed and was taken to the factory floor, given a curt cursory tour of the front of the factory, where the thimbles emerged from the kiln, ready to be glazed and fired. Then, wordlessly, I was taken into the back of the factory. It was filled with boxes and crates and bins of human bones, boiled and scrubbed and gleaming.

Across the room, two men shovelled the bones into a huge metal grinder where giant stone burrs crushed them into coarse powder. The powder was sent through a series of furnaces, sifted and combed and ground between each, until what emerged at the end was a trickle of fine white ash.

The Grazyn family had provided our livestock and

produce, chosen our grains, paid for our doctors and medicine, built and repaired our housing. They had given us our schooling, our training, our church, our cemetery. And not just for our village, but two others besides.

We all had been raised and fed and nurtured to become these bones.

"Sergyi was with the shovellers," my guide said to me in a dry, distant voice. "We need three, or we fall behind. You must take his post. Can you do the job?"

"I can," I said. I reached for the shovel hanging on a nearby hook—his shovel, I realized—and took my station, and went to work.

ALEXIA

I come from a line of seven mothers who were healers, *mudri materi*—women who detected and treated illnesses among the healthy, who ministered to the sick and the dying. Running our hands over the body, we could feel minuscule tumours, clots in the bloodstream, swollen or atrophied organs, irregular pregnancies, diseases in the glands and muscles and tissues and nerves and the brain. Some we could heal with touch, others with rough medicines, and a few with precise but painful surgeries. The rest we would recognize and respect as inevitable, inescapable afflictions to which one must gracefully surrender. These are old skills, invested with old knowledge, passed down through the centuries. And they come with a cost.

It is our tradition to assist all who ask, with no compensation expected. Still, the villagers have been generous over the years, and have given money, food, livestock—even the land and the house in which we have lived. They are not our kind, and they know our ways are not their own. They trust us, and fear us, without understanding us. *Tsyplyata*, my mother called them, which of course means chickens, and is not very polite.

One farmer brought us a goat because we had helped his wife through a difficult birth. My mother said, "You would take gifts from a chicken?" and I had to apologize to him because he had heard every word.

As for my own kind, well. Those of us who are descended from the old bloodlines, we have unusual anatomies and physical challenges. We can only seek help from our own.

The night that I was born, our house was struck by lightning. Our weather vane took all the shock; you could see a black halo in the grass where the charge went into the ground. The elder women saw it as a sign—they watched me closely for talents that I would need help in managing, they took me on visits and showed me the difference between one infection and another, between lumps that were harmless and those that were lethal. My mother saw that I was learning faster than she had, and she fed my appetite for knowledge even as she resented it.

I knew instinctively to conserve my talents, to watch the others and reveal less of myself. There were some people I knew I could not help, and others who needed little except common sense and compassion. My mother and grandmother could see so much in others, and yet I was opaque to them. They did not know what I knew, what I could do. I knew everything about them, and I struggled with that knowledge.

As was required by the tradition, neither I nor my mothers before me could marry—for any man who wed one of us would be cursed, as would be the marriage itself. My great-grandmother had defied the tradition—had met a young soldier, run away from the village, and married in secret. She became pregnant that night and the next day he was called into battle. She came back to her family, and everyone worried that the husband would be killed in the war. But it was worse. He came back alone, in the night, mauled and infected by a *strigoi*, not from among us but from somewhere in the north. Her husband was left monstrous and ravenous and incurable, and he could only be killed by a silver knife slashing his throat and genitals, held by his wife. She loved his *kochet*, and kept it in a jar and fondled it many times over the years. Its flesh lived while she lived, and died when she died. She never knew another man, and she never had another child.

When my turn came to bear a child, I visited the oldest man in the village, Yevgeny, who was very happy to see me. He was ninety-two, and while he had loved his life, he was ready to die.

"I have lived too long," he said to me, taking my hands in his. "What must I do?"

"Come with me," I told him, then led him to his bedroom, undressed him, let him undress me. Despite his age, he grew hard and thick in my mouth. I reclined with him on the bed, grasped him, helped him to enter me. He moaned, his wetness quickly flooded me. "What must I do?"

"Tell me you love me," I breathed as I held him close, "that you will make me your wife."

"I love you, I—I will make—" Then nothing, a whisper of breath. He was dead. And my daughter was soon to be born.

NICOLAI

I do not remember this. I cannot say what is true. A year after she and my father married, my mother lost her first child and was told there would be no other. This was hard as you can imagine, and my mother told my father to go and find another wife who could bear him a boy. My father loved my mother and remained. But their dead son was a shadow between them that even strangers could see.

The story she told: One day, just as winter was turning to spring, my father was helping a neighbour repair his barn while my mother stayed at home sewing. She heard a cry from the forest behind the farmhouse and, rather than wait for him to return, she went out to see what it was. Just beyond the line of the trees, still in sight of the house, she found me lying in the fresh-fallen snow, a baby, naked and shivering and close to death. No footprints anywhere. I had white hair and pale eyes. She thought I was her first son's ghost. She named me after him, nursed me as if she had borne me and, when no one came to claim me, she and my father made me their own.

But there were wolves in those woods, sometimes

heard but seldom seen. They howled, but did not come near. One evening, my father was out back with me, near the berry bushes. He looked up and saw a pack of dark hunched figures, with glittering eyes, watching from within the trees. He bundled me up, startling me into tears, and he hurried me into the house. He had a gun, his father's hunting rifle, but he had never killed with it, and my mother had never touched it. He took it down from the back closet shelf, stepped out the door and raised it. The dark figures and their shining eyes were already gone.

A few mornings later, my mother awoke to feel a cool breeze curling around her toes, the scent of fresh grasses filling the bedroom. She looked out into the hall to see the back door into the kitchen was open, sunlight bursting into the house. She gasped, jumped from the bed, checked my crib. I was gone. She screamed, waking my father, and pulling her clothes around herself she ran into the sunshine, blinded, shouting and crying, into the forest. She stopped just where the leaves cast their shade on the ground, and she stood and she looked and she listened. And my father stopped and stood beside her, holding the rifle.

It was quiet and still. Quiet as no forest should be.

"We will need help to search," he whispered. "We will need ten, maybe fifteen men."

"No," she hissed. "I will not leave. We must find him now."

She looked to the right, where a small rise was crowned with a trio of beech trees. She moved slowly towards it while my father watched—then stopped, listened again. A high light whine, and then gentle panting. She motioned for my father to come in closer; then she carefully crept to the source of the sound. In a den on the other side of the rise, a white wolf was nestled on a pile of rags, nursing her young: three tiny white pups, and me—the warm wolf milk smeared around my hungry mouth.

My father raised the gun—and my mother stopped him. "No," she said. And as the word spilled from her mouth, three other wolves emerged from among the trees. He lowered the barrel, and he and she moved backward slowly as the animals stared intently. Once out of the forest, my father turned and asked "What will we do?"

"We will wait," my mother said. "I will wait. They will not harm him, or they would have done so." Then she turned to my father and said, "She saw my face, and I saw hers."

"They are animals," he spat. "Our son, is he also an animal?"

"We are all animals," she answered. "I will wait."

The next evening, my mother was in the kitchen making supper, talking to my father in the other room when she realized she was alone. He had slipped out the door behind her. Suddenly she heard one shot, and then another. She rushed out to see him stagger out of the woods, and fall to the ground. She screamed and ran to him—his face and neck had been mauled, and he shuddered furiously, the blood coursing out of him and then slowing to a trickle. The convulsions slowed and stopped. He was dead.

A howl tore through the forest behind her. She turned and ran to the den to find a woman who was not a woman, a woman with long white hair and eight teats, shot in the shoulder, her pups bewildered and mewling around her, and around me. She saw my mother and pulled the rags over herself, which my mother saw were her blouse and skirt.

My mother went to her, knelt with her, tore her own skirt to clean and dress the wound. She fed the pups warmed goat milk. She went and fetched water and food as the three wolves watched and waited. She stayed through the night with the woman, came back with me day after day, until one day the den was empty. The wolves had moved on.

I do not remember. I cannot say what is true. But I do know this: when my mother died many years later, I knelt beside her bed and cried, and the wolves in the woods, they cried along with me.

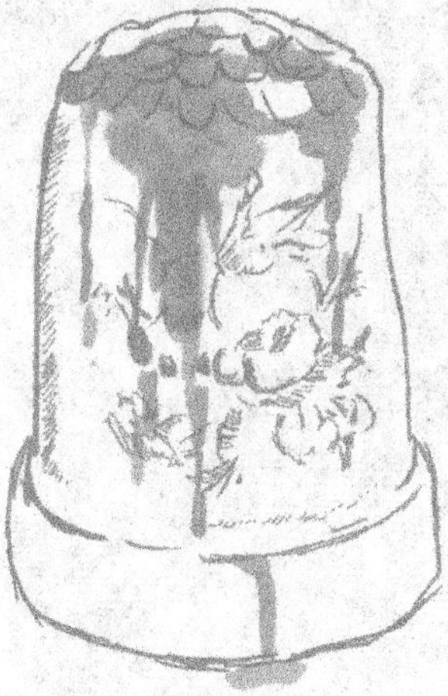

ROXANA

Mine was an ordinary childhood, until I was thirteen years old. As the chill of autumn crept over us and the first frosts wreathed the windowpanes, I discovered almost by accident that I had grown unaccountably strong, as strong as a man twice my size.

It was late afternoon, the air sharp with the promise of snow, and I was walking past the side road leading to the Malyks, two farms over. Their sons were on the side road kicking around an old leather ball. The older one, Lukas, two years older than me, he kicked the ball hard as I passed, perhaps to catch my eye and impress me as boys sometimes do. The ball soared towards me and without thinking I dropped my books and reached up and caught it. Their eyes went wide and I felt a hot rush of blood rise to my face. I had never seen a girl do this, and clearly neither had they.

The ball suddenly felt repugnant in my hands and I threw it too hard to get rid of it, sent it flying back at Lukas and knocked him down with it. The ball burst along one of its decrepit seams, spilling buckwheat everywhere. *It's not my fault*, I instantly thought. *The wind grabbed it and pushed it into him. And of course it burst, horrible old thing, the laces were already rotten, I could smell it when I threw it.*

But still.

Lukas stood up, rubbing his shoulder where he had been struck. He and his brother stared at me, then turned and ran home, the younger one clutching the ball to his chest like a mutilated animal.

When I came home, I said nothing, but went to the room that I shared with my five-year-old brother. I closed the door. "Sit on the bed," I told him. He did so. I stood at the foot, grabbed the old iron frame with both hands, and easily lifted it up over my head, nearly tipping him into the wall. Slowly and carefully, I lowered it back down till it touched the floor with only a creak.

"Don't tell anyone," I said sternly, and he nodded nervously.

Both the Malyk's farm and ours were well outside of town, and our families kept to themselves. Even so, as my parents and brother and I arrived at the village church on Sunday morning, it was clear that word of the incident with the ball had spread. The Malyk boys stayed well away from me, but some older boys came over to make a point of taunting me. "You should come play football with us, Roxana," one of them teased. "Our team might actually win a game for once."

"What's this about?" my father asked. "You playing games with boys?"

I realized he would hear about it anyway, so I told him as blandly as I could. "Lukas tossed his ball to me. I threw it back and knocked him down. It was nothing, an accident. I expect I injured his pride as well as his shoulder."

Before he could say anymore, we heard a shot, a horse's screech and a crash. We ran to the side of the church to where the carts and carriages waited, to find two of my father's friends running towards us. "Your son, your son! He is trapped!" Farther ahead we saw one of the traps had slid into the ditch by the road and fallen, its frightened horse still leaping and bucking as Mr. Malyk and several other men tried to calm it.

"Father," I said as I rushed to the side of the carriage, "help me lift it." He shook his head, stammered, looked to the other men—but they were all looking at us. "Father, put your hands on the carriage and help me."

Baffled at his friends and neighbours all standing back and staring, he numbly obeyed me and was stunned as, together, we lifted the carriage up. My brother crawled out crying, dragging his leg below the knee. My mother rushed to him, as did Mrs. Malyk and the doctor's wife, and the doctor himself joined soon after. The Malyk boys watched sullenly from the corner of the churchyard.

My father turned to Mr. Malyk, who had finally brought the horse back into rein. "What happened? What was the shot?"

A woman stepped up, Mrs. Derhak from the post office and general store. "I saw the whole thing," she said. "A pale young woman with long red hair, she grabbed your boy by the hand, she was trying to take him away. He was struggling but she had a dark power, she—I think she came from the river."

"A *rusalka*," said Mr. Malyk, and a shiver ran through the crowd. Many young women from the village had drowned in the river. It could have been someone's long-dead sister, daughter, wife. "I am the one who shot at her, but she threw your boy into the ditch and vanished. The shot spooked the horse, and the cart fell down onto him."

"A clean break," Dr. Krajnik said as he came to us. "I have dressed it for the moment, but we must take him to my office. We can use my carriage." He turned to me. "I'd also like to examine you, if I may. I think you know why." I nodded, and together we walked to the doctor's carriage, which stood parked at the head of the line. I peered in at my brother who was lying across two of the seats.

"I'm sorry," he said. "I wasn't supposed to tell."

Later, my mother and father argued while I held my brother in our room. Father was afraid: apparently some abnormal children in the eastern village had been taken by the authorities, for purposes unknown. For three weeks I was kept from school as my parents circled each other in a sour silence. Then, that last Sunday, as they took my brother to church but left me at home, I gathered my things into the small grey suitcase from under my mother's side of the bed, and I started walking west. I had seen handbills for a Turkish circus that was visiting Rakhiv. It would take me all day and into the night to reach it, but I no longer tired easily.

I remained with the circus for nearly two years. We travelled all over Europe. When our tour took us back towards my home, I asked if I could stop and visit. And then I was told, and wouldn't believe, and had to see for myself: in the brief time that I'd been away, my home, and my village, were gone.

LUISA

This was many years ago, back in the first land, when my grandmother was still alive and I was a small child. I would be sent to visit her in the woods, and while she was cooking she would tell me stories of the Bone Mother. *The little girl came up to the Bone Mother's house and knocked on the heavy wooden door. It opened all by itself and the little girl, who was very much like you, saw the Bone Mother at her giant wood stove. There she stood, throwing handfuls of vegetables in a big black pot made of iron, just like her teeth.* And then my grandmother would smile with her teeth made of iron, and I would giggle and shiver.

The Bone Mother lived in a little house deep in the woods, just like my grandmother's house, where she received visits from lonely young women, children cast out by their heartless parents, and handsome but treacherous men. The Bone Mother could be very wicked or very kind, and sometimes both. *Do all I ask and I will reward you. If not, I will eat you up.*

Once, as she was telling these stories, a whimpering came from one of the cages in the darkest corner of the kitchen—from one of her little *kurchas*, or chicks as she called them. Over she flew like a big black crow, pulled a little hand out of the cage and bit off one of its fingers. As the little *kurcha* screamed and screamed, my grandmother sat back on her stool, a thin trickle of blood dribbling down to her chin. "There," she said. "Now you have something to cry about."

I never looked too closely at the cages.

I would visit every Saturday, and always for lunch, and lunch was always a boiled egg, a bit of cheese, a bowl of potato soup, fresh-baked bread and some cold salted meat left over from the night before. She would watch me carefully as I ate, and in particular when I ate the meat, to make sure I finished everything she fed me. Once I eyed my plate suspiciously—the meat was so much like a tiny leg, with a tiny foot at the end and tiny little toes—and I asked her, "Are you the Bone Mother, Babcia?"

"I might be and I might not," she answered. "But I will tell you this: I am the oldest of our mother's daughters and, of all my children's children, you are the one who will one day take my place. You will live in my house, you will have all my jewels and gold. My cooking pots. My iron teeth. My many visitors. Some will come to you for wisdom, some for strength. Some will come with cakes and wine, asking for help to find true love or to seek revenge. Others will come to cheat and trick you, and even try to kill you. You must protect this house, and our families, and you must protect yourself."

"Why are you telling me this?" I asked. "Is something going to happen? Are you going to die?"

"Everything dies," she said simply, "and I am no different. One cannot be afraid. As you become a woman, my time will come to an end. And then, when you are very old, another in our line will take her turn."

"But the Bone Mother is a wicked witch who eats naughty children," I cried. Babcia smiled and pushed my plate closer to me, the little leg glistening in a sauce of butter and herbs. Nervously, I picked it up with my fingers and tore at the meat with my teeth. It was, admittedly, delicious.

"Good children do taste better," she said wistfully, "but there are so few of them. If you can be satisfied with naughty children, you will always have food on the table. They are never in short supply."

"But I don't want to be wicked, I don't want people to be afraid of me. I want to make them happy. I want them to love me."

She seemed hurt by this, and became very still, and the whole house grew quiet around her. "I wanted that too," she said softly. "We all want that at the start. You will see how the world changes you. Your kindness will be met with hate. Your wisdom will be met with fear."

I set the bones back down on the plate, stripped of all their flesh. I took a piece of thick white bread and wiped the juice from my plate, and from my chin. My grandmother's long thick tail, pink and hairless like that of a rat, unfurled from behind her and swept the bones into a bowl to be set aside for roasting.

"I cannot tell you how to be," she said, taking my hand. "You can only be who you are. But to be the Bone Mother is to always be hungry. What you eat, and why, depends on you."

Two full centuries have passed. I am now the oldest one. The little house is gone, as are the jewels and gold. I have outlived my own children and their children. Few from our families have survived, and those who did so fled to escape the enveloping darkness.

Yet among those few there is a child, one who will succeed me. She feels the gnawing in her belly and it draws her to my hiding place. For a time, we will dine together. I will tell her my stories, and teach her what she needs to know. Through her, our kind will live anew. I will not be the last.

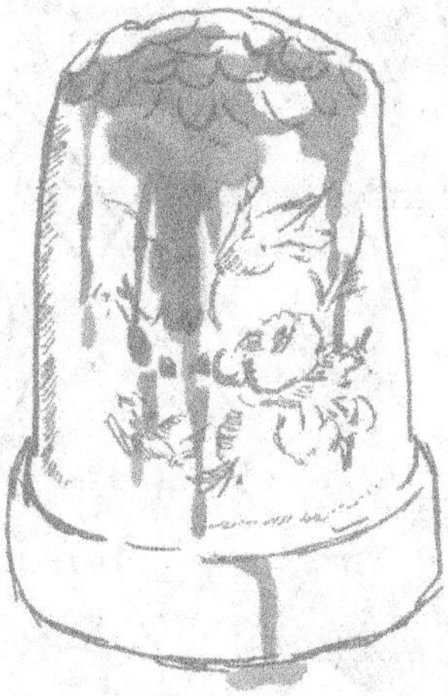

KATERINA

To get to my grandmother's house, if you don't drive, you have to take a westbound bus from Winnipeg that takes you through Brandon, Portage La Prairie, Gladstone, Neepawa, and finally to Minnedosa. From there you have to call Mr. Huliak who lives just outside of Sandy Lake, and he will come and pick you up. He's usually around, though you may have to try a few times as he doesn't always hear the phone. There's a coffee shop in Neepawa not far from the bus station. It used to be family-run, a place called the Wander-In, but now it's a Timmy's. Still, the women who work there have done so for decades, and they will remember you as Joe's daughter or Will's niece or the oldest of Nellie's grandchildren, the one from the city, pat on the cheek. Everyone knows who you are.

Then you sit with a double-double and a honey cruller encrusted in glaze and wait until Mr. Huliak pulls up in his primer-clad pickup. He won't step out or even wave, so you have to sit by the window and watch or, if it's summer, stand outside in case he comes up some funny way, from getting gas or something. Then you toss what's left of the coffee and cruller and hop into the passenger seat, and he'll say hello but not much else as he's never felt good about his English, though he understands you perfectly fine.

Then he'll drive up and over and down the curving road south of Riding Mountain, which is barely a hill if truth be told, through the lush greens of midsummer or the reds and golds of fall or the unsullied white of winter, till one more turn takes you to the top of the lane where he stops to let you off. You pull out a ten and insist that he take it, you know how things are up here on these farms. And he does. *Are you sure you're okay from here?* Yes, I'm good. Then a nod and he puts the truck into gear, pulls away and drives off.

Except this time, this one time, another voice answered, right on the first ring: a woman's voice, my age, a bit older, and weary. "Is Mr. Huliak there?" I asked.

"He died a few months ago," she said. "I'm his daughter, Riva. Who's this?"

This was so unexpected, I let out a little gasp, then caught myself, forced myself through the moment and apologized, said who I was, whose daughter I was. She sounded vague and uncomfortable, as if just up from a nap. I reminded her of our occasional meetings as children at one house or another, awkward lunches and teas in stiff flowered dresses when we'd rather have been playing outside.

"I see you now," she said—a funny phrase, as if she could tune me in like a radio, lock onto some weak signal and through it find my face. "Someone told me yesterday that your grandmother passed, I guess it didn't register. It's been a hell of a year. Were you wanting a ride out to her place?"

"Well," I said haltingly, "if you know someone that I could call—"

"I'll come get you," she answered. "It's all good, I have the truck, I should get some use out of it." I tried to talk her out of it but she was hard-headed like her father, and maybe a bit lonely, too. She was on her way out the door before I'd even hung up.

Mr. Huliak usually took twenty minutes to drive to the coffee shop, and Riva arrived just a few minutes shy of that, rounding the corner with a faint squeal and bump-bumping up into the lot. I could still see the five- six- and ten-year-old Riva in her flinty eyes and solid jaw, her lightly freckled nose and cheeks—she had a solid no-nonsense look about her, with some silvery grey threaded through her long dark hair. There shouldn't have been so much distance between us, but she had been in school when I wasn't and vice-versa; at those times when two girls could have grown closer, we drifted apart. Still, her face warmed slightly to see me, and I smiled in return. We were each glad to see someone who was neither a stranger nor a busybody.

I stepped into the cab of the truck and pulled the door shut behind me, gave her a light short "city hug" and asked "You know the way?"

"Pass it every day," she said, then pulled back out of the parking spot, spun the wheel and hit the gas.

To catch a ride with someone local from Minnedosa to Sandy Lake, and especially if you now live in the city, you first ask your driver about weather and the crops, who's alive and who's not, if anyone has left in the last few years and where they've gone, and who you might both know in Winnipeg, or Toronto, or out west in B.C. Even with friends or neighbours or family members, the ritual remains the same.

These conversations have different rhythms and rules from those that you have in the city, and settling into them can take some time. Some are just single words batted back and forth across the front seats.

"Josef?"

"Dead."

"How?"

"Pneumonia."

"Awful."

"Winter."

"Kids?"

"Gone."

"Sad."

"Mmm."

Others devolve into tangled monologues shot through with odd but telling details that hint at the causes, and the results, of otherwise inscrutable small-town behaviour. Bad debts, family fights, drunken brawls, police visits. After the city, and its relentless prying about your work, your parents, your home life, your curious singlehood—it's a relief to sit back and talk about other people, people who you know by name but not to speak to, people worse off than you, whose misfortunes are a welcome distraction from your own.

This time though, this one particular time with Riva, she asked as she was driving along the short stretch of highway, squinting against the sun: "Do you ever wonder what would happen if you just disappeared?"

I looked over at her and slowly shook my head, but confused—as if what she had said had come out all wrong, a puzzle I had to piece together. "I don't know what you mean," I said.

"Would anyone look for you, would you be missed?" She gave me a hard look that was almost a glare. "How long would it be before you were forgotten?" She turned away, gave that same hard look to the road ahead. "This stretch of highway, from here to Elphinstone, and down some of these side roads—over the last few years, maybe ten years or so—a dozen women, maybe more, just vanished. Women, and a few children."

"Women from town?" I managed to ask. "From the farms?"

"No," she said. "Just passing through, on their way from somewhere to somewhere. One time last year, I guess in the spring, still snow on the ground, they found a blue Honda on the shoulder up here. Baby seat in the back, everything buckled and fastened and locked. The mum and the baby were gone. Hood still warm. No one in sight. Cops were out here, the RCMP, flashlights in the fields and around all the outbuildings, knocking door to door. Never found them. All of them like that, over the years."

Riva fell silent for a moment, then asked again. “Well?”

“I don’t know,” I answered slowly. Words carefully chosen. “I like to think people would look for me. I like to think I’d be missed, that I wouldn’t be forgotten. Every time I go online now, I get one message or another—two years since so-and-so died, we miss him every day.”

“I don’t think there’s anyone that would miss me every day,” Riva replied. Not sadly, not sharply—just matter-of-fact. A tiny knot pulled tight in the pit of my stomach. And then: “Does anyone know you’re here?”

“Yes,” I said. “The estate lawyer. My co-workers. My ex. They all have names and numbers, including the coffee shop, including your dad’s. Which I guess means yours. Why?”

“No reason,” she said. “It’s always good to be cautious.” She suddenly veered into the shoulder and stepped on the brake, sending gravel and dust clouds everywhere. “Is this where he used to let you off?” I looked past her, and saw the road down to the farm, as familiar as an old friend’s face, then looked back at her and nodded. “Do you want me to drive you down?”

I shook my head. “No, that’s fine. The walk will do me good.”

“Fair enough,” she said. “Call me when you’re ready to head back. You can pay me then.”

I grabbed my bag, my light summer jacket, stepped out of the truck and watched her drive off. Between Minnedosa and Elphinstone. Highway and side roads—thirty miles give or take. Sandy Lake was along that stretch, and Newdale, too. Twelve over ten years didn't seem like that many. And "missing" could mean anything. Sometimes people just leave. Sometimes women just leave, and take their children with them. Sometimes people just vanish.

To get to my grandmother's house from the highway, you walk south down a long worn dirt road for about a mile, past low brush and long grasses and foxtails, when you reach a bend that tugs you back east, down a soft slope between two stands of huddled pines, until you reach the curved driveway, the garage, the house itself on the left, the chicken coop off to the side, and the barn and the old house, the first house, down a winding path through a thicket of brush speckled with Saskatoon berries. Your thoughts are bright and warm like the first sunshine after a long rain, and you know that when you're in sight of the kitchen, your baba will rush out to greet you, throw her arms around you, then usher you in and pull out dishes and plates full of sweet red beets and boiled eggs and cucumbers in vinegar that she always seems to have waiting. She'll fret and fuss over how thin you are, she'll ask about boys, she'll pat your hair and hold your hand—

But not this time. This time, I crossed the highway—pulling up my collar against the sudden chill. Frost can come even in June, killing things in the night that had only just struggled to the surface. I made my way down the long worn road that led to the farm, casting my eyes from side to side the way I did as a girl, looking for lost treasures. I reached the bend in the road, turned the corner, and as I drew closer I could see something ahead of me, something on the driveway, facing me as if to greet me or as if to warn me: a chair.

An old walnut chair, turned legs, back carved and sanded and softened with age, the seat covered in a threadbare cream and gold brocade, the grey flecked batting peeking through. A chair my grandfather had made, when he and his wife first settled here. A chair from the old house, the first house.

I stopped and stared at it, and it seemed to stare back at me. Confronting me.

Of course it was just a chair, but—why was it here, out in the open, exposed to the elements, at the end of the road? How long had it been here? I approached it, put my hand out to touch it—

—and as I reached out to grab the back, my hand passed through a warmth, a tenderness, a knowing. I let my hand linger—

—then pulled it back sharply, as if I had burned myself. The sharp cool country air snapped around it like a glove that had been left out in the snow.

Suddenly my cellphone vibrated in my pocket. I pulled it out and looked at the screen. A message from Riva, just one word:

RUN

A low rumbling hum caught my ear and I looked up the road to see a trio of cars, low and dark, no headlights, just making the turn towards me.

RUN

I rushed down the path through the bushes that led to the old house, shouldered the door, shoved and shoved, pushed my way inside, and then shut it tight behind me. I ducked down, peering through the old thickened glass as one by one the cars pulled up, their engines stilled, and a clutch of men in dark hats and long coats stepped out. Short words, sharp words, some English, some Russian. Men from the town? I couldn't see. One stared at the old wooden chair, just inches from the first car's front bumper. He kicked it aside. In the back seat of the second car, a woman, gestured at, shouted at, told to stay—or to get out? I couldn't tell. She looked down as if she hadn't heard, but didn't move. Strands of grey glistening in the afternoon sun. I knew who that woman was.

After my father and his brothers had helped my grandparents build the new house, the old house—just one large room with the window and door facing east—became first a henhouse and then a storage shed, stacked with old wood and baling wire, rusty tools hanging on rusty nails, shelves cluttered with tins filled with cup hooks and screws and hinges and tacks, piles of mouldering books and papers and photos and old wooden pull toys. A blue plastic monkey, long lost from the barrel of its brothers and sisters. A thick layer of dust coated everything. Cobwebs hung from the struts of the ceiling. Every corner was webbed and strung with little gnarled bodies. I dared not look too closely.

We were forbidden from coming in here and, while of course we disobeyed, we only snuck in two or three times that I could remember. We never felt comfortable in here—cold and dark and damp, squat and forlorn, it was the new house's melancholy older sister. We called it the ghost house. But now it was the haven, the sanctuary, clutching me breathless to its breast. In one motion, all of the men reached into their coats, pulled out and cocked their blunt black pistols—and then stopped, interrupted, as one waved to the others, shushing and gesturing downward. He had heard something. Now they all could hear it. And then, so faintly, I could hear it too. Someone, a woman, humming or singing inside of the house, to herself or to a small child. Just a few notes in, I began to whisper along. It was something my mother had sung to lull me to sleep.

Bayu-bayushki-bayu
Nye lozhisya na krayu
Pridyot serenkiy volchok
I ukhvatit za bochok
On ukhvatit za bochok
I potashchit vo lesok
Por rakitovyi kustok

Baby, baby, rock-a-bye
On the edge you mustn't lie
Or the little grey wolf will come

And he will bite you on the bum
Tug you off into the wood
Underneath the willow root

As the men listened, they moved off of the driveway, into the yard, onto the steps, through the door and one by one into the house, as if the tune was winding itself around them and drawing them in.

And then I saw her. The tall sheer curtain at the side of the dining room window shivered, and she stepped out from behind it, perfectly framed, looking towards the front hallway, facing the intruders who were just out of sight. It was odd—I could see her, but not quite see her, my eyes unable to focus. And all this time singing, singing. And then all in a moment, her hair, her face, her body, her clothing, they all at once came together and—

—*it's me*, I thought, *oh my God it's me, that's me in the house, in the window, it's me*, and the woman raised her hand—

A shot. And a thud.

Again. And again. Six men. Six shots. Six thuds. And then she laughed, a light bell-like laugh that stung my ears, and disappeared from view.

The dining room window shattered. Towards the back of the room, down near the floor, a creamy golden light began to flicker and spread. Within minutes, the house was engulfed in flames.

I looked over at Riva, brushing away the tears that were shimmering on her cheeks. She sat in the car and watched the house, watched the door. When it was clear that no one would ever emerge, she moved from the back seat to the front. Turned the ignition. Put the car into gear. Then slowly made her way back up the road to the highway.

Once I knew she was gone, truly gone, I pulled open the door of the old house, the ghost house, then shut it tight behind me, stepped into the sharpening air, walked up the path through the brush, picked up the old walnut chair, righted it and sat on it, and watched the new house burn. It had begun to collapse in on itself, sprays of sparks shooting upward as timbers fell, as the roof buckled, as the floors gave way. To burn a house takes no time these days—half an hour, an hour at the most, much less than a hundred years ago. So much plastic now, and the wood all thin and light and crisp like kindling. Even this house, new in name only, took just a few hours to surrender completely, to crumple and curl as the moon edged up into the sky.

Nichni Politsiyi. Words I remembered from my earliest days here. My grandfather sitting in this chair, in that window, all through the night. I was five, I think, or six, and we had come to visit for Easter weekend, though we never went to church. Funny that. But I remember getting up out of my bed, late in the night or early in the morning, ever so quiet, creeping into the hall, my hand lightly touching the wall, my bare feet softly padding along the floor, and my grandfather's whisper from the dining room: "Who's there?"

And I whispered: "Me, Papa—where are you?"

And he said softly: "Come have some water and go back to bed."

And I crept around the corner into the dining room and there he was, in this chair, in the window, in the dark. Sitting and watching. He had a glass of water for me. I took it and drank it, set the glass down.

"Now go to sleep," he said.

"Why are you here?" I asked. "What are you looking for?"

"Nichni Politsiyi," he answered, and then: "It's not for you to worry about. Go back to your room and sleep."

"I want to watch with you," I told him, but he shushed me and turned me and gave me a pat on the rear.

"Off with you," he said. "And let us hope we never ever see them."

But now I had.

By the time I was old enough to ask who they were, what they wanted, no one would say. My mother, standing at the sink, clattering plates and bowls and cutlery as she washed the dishes, pretended not to hear me and when I pressed the case, she turned and hissed, "That's enough." Then stopped, and slowly lifted her hand from the water—something had broken, a glass or a jar, her palm was slashed across the lifeline and the blood was streaming through the white soapy froth down to her wrist. I pulled an old tea towel from the front of the stove and she pressed it to the wound and sighed once more, almost to herself, "That's enough."

I look back now and realize: our family lived in fear.

My parents, my grandparents, they came to this new land and brought their fears with them, and they underscored everything like the faint, staticky hiss on my grandfather's old Riga radio. At a time, when our neighbours thought nothing of leaving their doors unlocked, ours were checked every night and every morning, and the windows, too.

Never walk into a dark room, we were taught. Always look in the car's back seat. Never cross a strange animal's path. Always know where the door is and keep your left eye trained on it. My father's youngest brother died before I was born, just a teenager, he fell down a well. These things happen on farms, farms are dangerous places. Something like this, no one sees or hears you, your life slips away while parents, brothers, neighbours scour the property calling for you. Your name being shouted far above your head by ever more frantic voices, your name formed out of cries and sobs, this becomes the last sound you hear.

The second youngest, handsome and studious and possibly gay, died in a one-person car accident when I was ten, just lost control of his car and flew off through a guardrail and down a fifty-foot drop. Cool clear night, starlit sky, not another vehicle for miles. "Untimely accidental demise," said the obituary, unconvincingly. Suicide, my mother said one night when I was listening on the stairs, but my father just sat silent.

And as I sat in the old wooden chair watching the new house succumb to the flames, I wondered what had really happened, to both of them, if there was something more.

When I was a little girl, we would drive back from my aunt's in Elphinstone well after dark. There was one short stretch where the road dipped and rose like a roller coaster, and my dad would turn off the headlights and we rolled rolled rolled in the pitch-darkness and my mother would cry, "Don't do that, you're scaring the children!" when, of course, we loved it and she was the one who was scared. But after Uncle Ted died, we always drove that stretch slowly with the lights on full so we could see the road ahead and everything on it.

I stood up from the old walnut chair and approached the house, peered into what had been the dining room. The furniture, of course, was destroyed, and small fires still burned here and there, but the floor on this side was more or less intact. I could see the shattered window glass, the six charred bodies. The bullets, gleaming in the firelight. Had they shot themselves? Or each other? And who, or what, had lured them in?

Oh my God, it's me, it's me—

I wrapped my scarf around my right hand, reached up and into the ruin, picked up one of the bullets and looked at it closely. A tiny stamp into the metal along one side, a sword pointing down behind a crescent moon. I gently dropped it back on the floor where I found it, then turned back, started walking back, back towards the berry bushes, the winding path. I had seen that stamp somewhere before, somewhere in the old house, the ghost house, and now I wanted to see it again.

At the bottom of the path I stopped, stood still and silent. The old house's old grey door was wide open.

I switched on the tiny blue-white flashlight on my phone and peered inside, stepped inside. It was unexpectedly warm, and dry, dust hanging in the air like a fog. I was alone, and yet—and yet—it was as if someone was behind me, around me, lightly lifting my arm, turning my hand, shining the light onto the papers and photos in the corner. I went to them, knelt before them, reverently, but without yet knowing why. One of the pages partway down the pile was turned so that a small round insignia at the top was revealed. Black and white, yellow and red, the sword and the crescent moon. I lifted the pages, went to pull out the one and saw that beneath, and above, were many similar pages. Forms of some kind, typewritten in Russian, with names and dates and in some cases small photos. Male, female, families, children. Some had letters and numbers stamped, some had handwritten scrawls. Each was dated and signed at the bottom—1939, 1940, 1942, 1938, 1936. Most from during the war, but some from before.

Thirty-seven. Who were they?

As I gathered them up, I saw one more, away from the piles of paper and photos, peeking out from under a crate in the corner. I tugged it out, held it up, to the light of the phone. I couldn't read any Russian, didn't recognize any of the other names, but this one I knew. Ковальчук. Kowalchuk. My grandmother's name. And stapled at the side, my grandmother Lexi's frightened young face.

Just then, my phone buzzed and buzzed, almost leaping out of my hand, as a cascade of text messages flew by. All from Riva, all from hours before.

I TOLD YOU TO RUN WHY DIDN'T YOU RUN
oh god i'm sorry i'm so sorry
Those men i don't know them they're friends of my fathers they just came out of nowhere i
Are you there?
The phone rang for a second, I don't know if that was you or
Are you there?
Are you alive?
What happened in there?
If you're there, if you're somewhere, say something anything
A word a letter
Anything

I thought for a moment, then texted back:

I am in the old house

Three grey dots appeared on the screen, pulsing back and forth. She was typing.

What old house?

I typed back:

The ghost house.

A long pause, and then the three dots again.

> *The ghost house is gone, it's been gone for years. It burned down when we were six. It's all overgrown now, nothing is there.*
> *Katerina? Is this you? Where are you?*

The ghost house had burned down. Of course I knew this. Sons crash cars and fall down wells, and houses burn. People vanish. These things happen on farms. I reached out to touch the wall in front of me. My fingers pressed against old grey wood—and then gently through it, its particles redistributing like tiny flies around my fingers. The wall was made of ash. The door, the roof, the crates, the books, the piles of paper and photos, all of it ash, grey upon grey upon grey. The evening breeze rose and swept through the old house, sending the ashes skyward, a swarming cloud of soot that spread high and wide, thinning until it vanished. I looked around and found myself kneeling in a patch of clover where the eastern wall of the house had been. Everything was gone.

> *Katerina?*

Confused, I absently scratched at my arm, which was hot and itchy and sore. I looked down and saw that my skin there was cracking, peeling, flaking. And underneath, a red-orange glow, like coals in a furnace, like embers, like lava. The more I scratched, the more my flesh fell away, and the brighter the orange glow burned.

I could not stay any longer. I now knew—I can't say how—that while these men were dead, more were on their way.

I'm coming, I texted back to her. *I'll see you soon.*

To get to the Huliaks' from my grandmother's house, you have to cut through the western field, which over the years has been seeded with barley, alfalfa, and hay, but these last few years has been resting, replenishing, before the cycle begins anew. Even so, you walk along the southern fence to the edge of the Huliak property, look north towards the outbuildings and past them to the main house, long and low and suburban, with a faint light coming from within. We always walked this way as children, west and north from fence to fence to gate to path, telling the stories that we'd been told and singing the songs that we'd been taught.

Here is a story we tell our children. Perhaps you were told this, too. Two sisters, twins, were born to a woodsman and his wife—but the woodsman had chopped down the oldest tree in the forest, a sacred tree, and so a witch of the wood cursed his daughters. Hana was made of fire and could burn you if you touched her. Gerda was made of ice and could freeze away your fingers. And of course, Hana and Gerda could never touch each other or they would both die.

The wood witch had a kind and powerful sister who heard the cries of the woodsman and his wife. She could not lift the curse, but she took the ice-child

Gerda to raise as her own and keep her apart from the Hana the fire-child. As she grew older, the wood witch befriended Hana the fire-girl and persuaded her that a more powerful and terrifying witch was holding her long lost sister captive. Because she didn't entirely trust her new friend, Hana began to drop secret notes in the woods for Gerda to find, and one day Gerda answered them with a note of her own, telling the truth.

Furious, Hana burned the wood witch's house to the ground, killing her—but also ensuring the curse could never be broken. Gerda saw the smoke above the trees and went running for her sister, but before the kindly witch could stop her, she rushed into Hana's arms, embracing her. The fire-sister Hana melted the ice-sister Gerda, and the water as Gerda melted turned Hana into ash. At the last moment, the kindly witch turned them both into flowers—the small red and white flowers known as Snow of the Mountain and Fire of the Valley that you find tangled together in the forests of the Old Country. In this way the sisters live on as the flowers live on, and through the story we tell.

I'm coming. The sun had long ago dropped from the sky, but the moon was high and bright above. And as I walked from fence to fence to gate to path, my skin now falling in tatters from my incandescent body, my radiant arms outstretched, thousands of tiny red flowers sprang up behind and around me, night-blooming in my wake.

I'm cutting through the field, Riva.
I will see you soon.

KRISZTINA

I am the girl in the water. I am the *rusalka*.

One day when I was thirteen, I woke up very ill, so tired that I could not get out of my bed to go to school. Mama felt my head, listened to my chest. I had no fever, no cough, my heart was strong. I was a good student and rarely unwell, so she kept me home, but I could see she was concerned. At lunch I could eat very little, the smell of everything was overpowering to me. I was sick all over myself and again in the sink. Finally she warmed some clear broth for me and brought it to my bed.

"Mama," I said. "I have a fish in me."

It was as if she didn't hear me, so I said it again, and louder. "Mama. I have a fish in me. The fish is making me sick." And I took her hand and pressed it to my belly. The little fish quivered and curled under her hand, and she pulled it away as if she had burned herself.

"How did this happen?" she asked, frightened and furious. "Who has done this to you?"

I was confused, I didn't know what she meant. "I don't know, I don't know," I insisted, now as afraid as she was.

She slapped me across the face. "Have you let any boys touch you or kiss you?"

My cheek was stinging, my eyes were wincing with tears. I didn't like boys, never played with them at school or after, ran and hid and waited for them to pass whenever I could. And then I had a thought, not knowing it was the worst thought of all.

"Mama," I said. "Could a woman have put the fish in me?"

She became very still. "What do you mean?" she whispered.

"When Papa was out in the field," I said, "and you were at the church with Mrs. Derhak, a woman I didn't know came to the door, an old woman, and she wanted to play a game with me, and she said I shouldn't tell you or we would all get into trouble. She said it would be a game but—all I remember was she held my hands up with one hand and tickled my belly with the other, and I laughed and I laughed until I fell asleep, and then when I woke up she was gone."

After a long moment, with her face turned away from me, she said "I see."

I waited and waited. The little fish was whirling around inside me, as fearful as I was. But she sat and sat on the edge of my bed and then finally asked, "Have you ever seen this woman before? In the village? On someone's farm?"

"No," I said.

"Only this once?" she asked.

"Yes," I said.

She turned to me, and somehow her face was so

dark that I could barely see it, even though the sun had yet to slip down and out of the sky. "Come then," she said, "you must get dressed. I know how we will make you feel better."

She bundled me out of the house while I was still wrapping my cloth coat around me. The fish was frantic now, swimming in tight wild circles, and the sickness and weakness were like heavy hands pulling at my shoulders, my legs, my hair.

"Please, can we go tomorrow?" I asked, but it was like shouting into the wind. She led me through the field to the path into the woods, which I knew eventually would lead to the lake. I knew there were plants you could eat, herbs and flowers and mushrooms that could take your sickness away. I had heard many stories of Baba Yaga, and the children at school often said that such witches still lived among us. Perhaps that was where she was taking me. Or perhaps she was a witch herself.

I struggled to keep up with my mother, whose stride had become broader and more purposeful as we emerged from the woods. The large cold lake stretched out before us. Soon we were at the water's edge. She pulled the coat from me, pushed me towards the water and said, "Go in."

"But it's so cold," I cried, and it was true—I could see my breath between us and knew the lake would be liquid ice.

"Good," she said. "The cold water will tighten around you and the fish will swim out, and you will feel much better. Go in."

Sick and cold and tired and sore, I obeyed her and stepped into the water. "Come over here where it's deeper," she said, "and put your hands up here on this edge." Soon the cold clear water was up to my chest, my neck, I held on to the edge and looked up at her.

"How long?" I asked. "How long?" I was shivering so hard I could barely hold on, my teeth were chattering.

"Not long," she said, kneeling down to me; then she reached out and grabbed a fistful of my hair and pushed me under the water. I tried to fight, I tried to struggle, but I could not. My final breath bubbled out of me, and soon even the little fish was quiet and still. Mama gently let go of my hair, and I sank to the lake's dark floor.

Then she screamed.

"Noooooo!" she screamed. "Noooooo!" And soon some men ran from the church, which was not far away.

"Mrs. Malyk!" they shouted. "What is it?"

"My baby, my Krizstina—she ran in the water and threw herself in—she was too fast, I tried to catch her!"

I looked up and saw the men peering over the edge, but I was too deep for them to see me. Suddenly, I felt the little fish quiver and curl inside me again, felt it flicker and warm me like a tiny red flame. The heat spread through me to the tips of my fingers and the ends of my toes. My body grew long and lithe, my breasts full and rounded. My hair, now long and lush and red like oxblood, eddied and swirled around me.

I swam out into the centre of the lake, then spiralled

up to the surface—looked across to where the cluster of men now poked at the water with long sticks and hooks. Even though it was impossibly far, I saw Mama, saw her face, and I fancied she saw me.

And then I turned and I dove down
down and

down

LORINCZ

The first time Luda came to visit, I was four years old, and so was she. I woke in the middle of the night to find her sitting at the foot of my bed.

There was something odd about her, misshapen. She was tiny and naked, more like a baby bird, a hatchling, than a girl. She held her knees up under her chin, one arm around her thin frail legs, and she was staring at me. I didn't know who she was, or how she had gotten into our house, into my little room off from where my mother and father slept.

Suddenly, she looked up at the window next to the bed, startled, as if something just outside was about to reach in for her—and then she vanished. From where I lay, I could only see moonlight streaming through the gently rustling leaves. I decided I wouldn't say anything to my parents, as they had no patience for stories or imaginings.

I woke up late, which was unusual. I was often the first out of bed. My mother wondered if I was ill. I felt a bit warm, and oddly sore. She lifted off my nightshirt and asked, "What have you done to your shoulder? Did you fall while you were playing? Did somebody hit you?"

I shook my head. She turned me so my father could see. “It could be a spider bite. Check the sheets to see.” Then with a slight smile he added: “I hope he didn’t swallow it.”

“Don’t put thoughts into the boy’s head,” my mother said sharply. It was too late. The thoughts were already there.

She prepared to corner Dr. Pavel at church the next day, but the welt faded over the course of the afternoon and by bedtime it was all but gone. Still she found him after the service and he took me to his office at her insistence, my shirt and jacket half off under the bright light over his metal table while he poked and prodded. Nothing. He shrugged, and I pulled my shirt back up. She frowned, and my father sighed in a what-did-I-tell-you way, or in a now-we-are-late-for-lunch way. I reached up under my collar, placed my fingers over the spot. Something deep under it curled on itself. *I hope he didn’t swallow it.*

Three years later, the welt returned, and so did Luda. This time there was blood, a spot of blood on the inside of my undershirt, as if I had scraped a wart or a mole. Not enough to soak through to the bedsheets, but enough that my mother’s eye caught it while I was dressing for school.

“What have you done there?” she asked. She pushed at it, and a droplet of blood welled up. She wiped at it with an old cleaning cloth that smelled of alcohol. She pushed again—something was under the surface, something hard like a sliver, a stone. She pushed and wiped, pushed and wiped, and up came something white and smooth, and out it popped, onto the red of the blood on the cloth. A chip of bone.

"I can't say for certain what it is," said Dr. Pavel, "or how long it's been there." He looked at my shoulder, which was pink and sore from all my mother's efforts. The wound, however, had begun to heal. He brushed on some mercurochrome, taped a square of gauze over it.

"Lorincz, you get dressed and wait here. I'm just going to talk to your mother outside." Her brow furrowed as he led her out the door, and it was still furrowed when Dr. Pavel returned and told me I could go. In the meantime, I had taken the tiny fleck and pocketed it in my handkerchief. It went into the little tin of treasures on my bookshelf.

My mother said little as we walked the three streets over to our house, and said even less at the dinner table. My father's various questions were answered with a single word: "After." Once I was in my room, and my father had closed the door behind me, I could hear my mother unleash all the other words she had been holding in. I struggled in vain to hear what she said, but her emotions were all too apparent: anger, and sadness, and fear.

That night, I awoke to find Luda once again at the foot of my bed. She seemed older now, though not much bigger. Once again naked and clutching herself, once again staring at me. This time, however, a thin trickle of blood flowed over the edge of her lip and down to her chin.

A tooth, I realized. *The tiny fleck was a tooth.* Just

then, she looked up at the window, startled as she had been before, and once again she disappeared. I realized I had heard one word from my mother's diatribe, and that word was "twin."

When I was twelve, just a few days after my birthday, I fell ill with a terrible fever. I was drenched with sweat, yet chilled to the bone. Overnight, the welt had returned, as large and round as a boil. Dr. Pavel had retired from his practice the year before, but he came at my mother's urging and he brought a woman from the next village, a *mudri materi*. While my mother cried in the other room, Dr. Pavel turned me on my chest, took out a scalpel and sliced into the boil. With a pair of forceps he carefully nudged around and pulled out four, five, six tiny bones and a little skull. After that, the *mudri* stopped him.

"Enough,"she said. "She is not an infection. She is not a parasite. The boy holds the blood and flesh of two people in one body. She is changing him, and we must not fight that change." She took my hand, and held it. "She will not let him die. He is her way into the world." The *mudri* watched as Dr. Pavel cleaned the wound and sewed it shut. And then he left so she could speak to me alone.

"You are very brave, and very strong," she said. "And so, too, is your sister. She is with us now. She is hurt and afraid. But she means you no harm. Do you see her sometimes?" I nodded. "Does she frighten you?" I shook my head. "Good. When you see her, you must welcome her, even if her appearance disturbs you. You will come to love her in time." And then she placed her hand on my forehead, and I felt the fever melt away.

I am twenty now, at school in Kolomyya, far away from home. Luda is with me always, like a deeply held secret, as close as my breath. Freed from her bones, she is soft and round, her arms and legs coiled around her head, a wreath of flesh framing and cradling her face. Her mouth open, her eyes wide, her tongue, her toes, her fingers, her breasts, her belly, her *kiska*, her eyes, her beautiful eyes. I feel her in every part of me. I look in the mirror and she is all I see.

CLAUDIU

It's not much, this little gift I have. I used it mostly in school when I was younger, just a lad, to scare the girls and sometimes the teacher, who would get angry and make me stand by the outhouse as punishment. Everyone in the school could see me from the window. She only had to do that twice and I never played my pranks again. Also, she spoke to my mother and I caught hell from her. That did the trick.

The gift is this: I can picture a small thing—a mouse, a snake, a frog—and I can send that picture with my mind so that everyone can see it. I can look along the floor and everyone will see the mouse running and then they'll jump up and scream. Not for long, my magic mouse, and not very far, just for a few moments and only for a metre or two. Or I can picture a frog, and make it hop from desk to desk. Or a snake on teacher's chair. That was the last time. I nearly got sent home for good. But my father was from one of the first families, so there was not much they could do. Still, I had to be careful, and so I stopped using the gift and after a time forgot it. Until one day, when I was older. I wondered if I could project a person. And it turned out I could. Not for long, and not moving at all. Just standing and staring, for a few seconds. And then it would vanish.

As I say, not much of a gift, not compared to some others. Not compared to my father, and some of his brothers. So I let it fall away into the past and become a distant memory.

When I was sixteen, my father died, at the factory, as was known to happen from time to time. The owner sent a car to us, sleek and black, with a crisp young man in a black suit bearing a letter.

Father had been forty-five, with only three months left in his requirement there. Management was very kind and waived the remainder of his contract. While I was technically old enough to fulfill it, I was not physically capable, nor was my mother. Another worker from our village had volunteered to substitute. We would receive my father's full pension. However, as was the custom, the funeral and burial would be held at the factory. We were to pack a change of clothing and then join the young man in the car for the drive back. We would be assigned special rooms that were reserved for bereaved relatives, then we would dine with my father's supervisor and his closest friends, and in the morning we would attend the ceremony.

We only had one black tin trunk between us, but that was enough. My mother brought out a somber blue dress and a sheer grey scarf printed with wine-coloured roses. I packed the suit that Mr. Koltusky, the village tailor, had made for me just six months before. It came with a white shirt, new black shoes and a grey silk tie. The tie was the most beautiful thing I owned, and there were nights when I would get up and go to the closet to run my thumb over it. I couldn't imagine a time when I would wear it, and now such a time had arrived.

My mother snapped the trunk shut and I lifted it off of the bed. We pulled on our thick woollen coats, stepped out and into the waiting car. The young man looked at my bare head, took his hat from the seat next to him, placed it on me. It was a smart fit, and he gave an approving nod. We were on our way.

The dinner was largely silent. It turned out that my father's supervisor and closest friends barely knew him at all. We learned that he had been an underglaze painter, a true artist, and not the labourer that I had envisioned. It was solitary work, and that solitude had extended beyond the factory floor. The meal itself was a mild meat stew—pork, I supposed—with white beans, root vegetables and potatoes. The men barely touched it. One shed tears throughout. After dinner we were shown to our rooms, which were modest in size but well appointed. I undressed and slipped into bed, and soon fell into a sound and dreamless sleep.

Shortly after dawn, a tap at the door roused us and we were called to breakfast. We dined alone on eggs and fried cabbage, and then were led through a courtyard where all of the factory's workers stood. Most stared down at the ground but a few stray eyes followed as we walked to a little chapel at the corner of the compound. Inside was my father's coffin, oak with simple mouldings but still more expensive than we could have purchased ourselves.

After a moment, the same men from the night before came in to join us in prayer and act as pallbearers. They carried the coffin out to a snug square graveyard just outside the gate, and lowered it into its freshly dug plot. As the men shovelled behind us, we were handed our black tin trunk, a certificate of my father's service and a box of his belongings. We stepped back into the sleek black car and were driven back to our home. As I looked out the window at the passing countryside, I wondered why the casket had been closed, and why it had seemed several inches shorter than it should have been. But I said nothing.

A few nights later, while we ate our supper, my mother looked at me and said: "I want to see him again. Please. You can still do that—can't you?" I nodded, then turned towards a chair in the corner, After a moment, there he was, sitting with us, watching us. I held him there as long as I could.

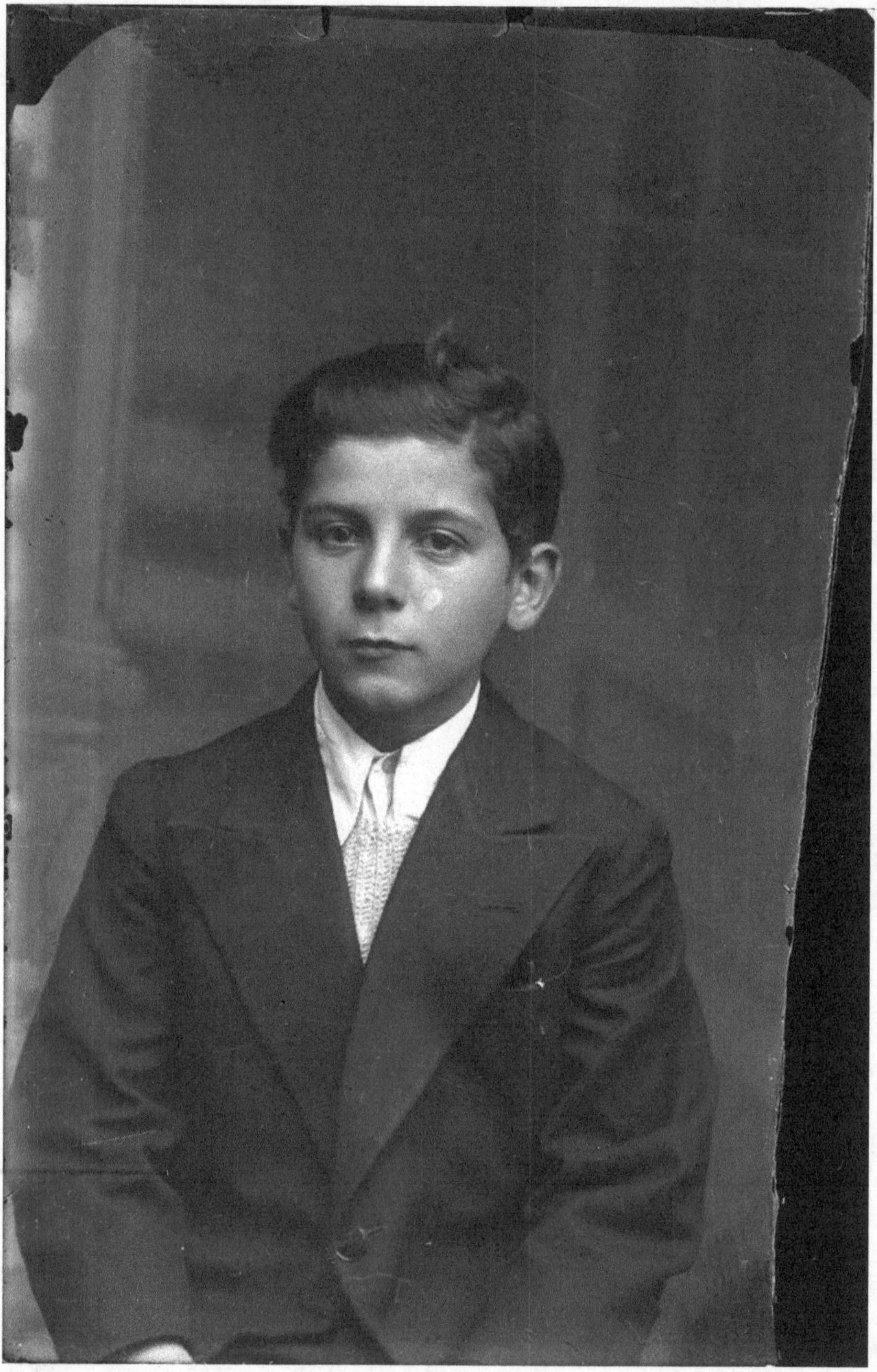

ANDREAS

When I was very small, just two or three years old, I remember my older brother Jerzs being scolded for daring to go with his friends near the old Borowycz house, which was down a winding lane on the way from our farm to the village school. Elderly Mrs. Borowycz was still alive back then, but whatever else lived there was no longer under her control. She would not be able to help anyone who fell prey to it, in the house or on the grounds. My brother pretended to laugh off his childish trespassing but it was clear to me that he had seen something that had frightened him. He did not need a warning not to return.

When I turned seven, it fell on him to walk with me to school. I told him I wanted to see the house. He of course refused, but I insisted, and said that I would tell our parents that he had taken me. He hated me in that moment, and said he would only walk me to the top of the lane and wait as I hurried down, saw the house, and came back. He would wait just ten minutes, as measured by our father's old military wristwatch, and then would leave without me. Ten minutes seemed like very little time, but I agreed.

"Go on, then," he said, and gave me a little push. Even in bright sunlight the path seemed dark and dire, lined on either side with frail withered trees whose life seemed to be leaching away even as the fields and forests surrounding were lush and teeming. "Ten minutes." He showed me the watch, the second hand click-click-clicking. I took a breath, pulled my right foot back to launch myself forward, and raced away.

The shadowed lane had unexpected dips and curves and a few times narrowed till it was barely a path, overgrown at the edges with tall scraping weeds that clung as I raced by. It felt like the full ten minutes had passed and my sides were beginning to ache when the house reared up as if out of nowhere, and I stopped and gasped and stared at it.

It was, in truth, a small and quite ordinary structure, with its steep roof, shingled walls and small dark windows. Mrs. Borowycz had died the year before, but it was as if the house had been abandoned for decades. I stood a moment more and then turned, prepared to rush back, when a slight movement caught the corner of my eye, as if a curtain in a window had stirred in the cool morning breeze.

It was not a curtain, though. In one window at the side of the house stood a boy, a boy who looked just like me—as if instead of a window, I was looking into a mirror. *Come*, he mouthed to me.

I ran.

I ran and ran up the lane, bounding over roots and puddles that I couldn't recall encountering on the way down. I saw that face, that mouth, *Come*, and an icy finger ran from the base of my skull down to the bottom of my spine. I ran and ran and ran and stopped at the top of the lane, but my brother Jerzs was gone. So I kept running, sweating and panting yet so very cold, *Come, Come*, until I reached the school and found my brother standing outside.

"You were late," he said. And then asked, "What did you see?"

"Nothing. A house. I saw nothing." He looked at me, disbelieving. And then the teacher rang the final bell, and we hurried inside.

Come.

The next morning, I woke up early, an hour before sunrise, slipped out of bed and into my clothes and walked up the road and down the lane until I once again faced the house. And the boy.

He was there again at the window, so pale he gleamed in the fading moonlight. He retreated into the darkness. I stepped up to the door, pushed it open. He was standing on the stair. "Who are you?" I asked. He spoke and I could feel the words curl into a black knot in my mind.

"We don't have long," he said. "I have some things to show you." He started up the stairs, and I followed him, reached up and took his cold small hand. And when we were done, I came back down, hurried up the path and back home before I was missed.

Many things died in the village that year, and in the farms around it. Small animals, birds, beheaded and gutted. A dog, a sheep, throats slashed. Two chickens, a foal. A baby went missing, just six weeks old, stolen out of its crib. Then a four-year-old girl, flung in a ditch, struck from behind and then smashed with a stone until her face caved in.

My brother saw me that one morning, saw me creep up naked and bloodied in the early light, watched me wash myself clean with the rainwater gathered near the back door, stared as I slipped into the house, into my bed, held my finger to my lips. Shhhh. He wouldn't walk with me that day, ran away from me as soon as he could. I walked along the road towards the school alone. As I reached the lane, I heard the whisper once again in my ear, and I knew the girl had been found.

I walked up to the house, I opened the door, I closed it behind me. I climbed the stairs, entered the room where the boy had shown me so many things. I lifted the board in the floor where I kept all our treasures. I slipped underneath and pulled it down over me, and I lay there and I waited.

I'm waiting there still. I'm waiting for you.

Come.

YEVGENY

Some stories need to be told time and again. Every generation forgets. Every child learns anew. These borderlands are contested ground, and have been for centuries. The lines between countries move north, then south, then north, then disappear for decades only to return again. Sometimes the war is at our doorstep. Other times, we do not hear of our new ruler until an army comes demanding payments or shelter or recruits. They take our food, our horses, our strongest boys, leave rubbish and bastards in their wake. Before this land even had a name. It has always been this way.

From time to time, they come to torture and to kill, to drive some of us out or march us away. Soldiers, militias, secret police. The uniforms change but the intent is the same. *Ochistka granits*, the cleansing of the borders. The Lemkos, the Rusnaks, the Poles. The Yevrei, of course, forced to hide and flee and renounce and convert, and even then still facing death. For many, these lands, these villages are the last refuge. Or else on the hillsides like the Hutsuls and the Boikos.

Here is a story that I can tell you. My mother

and father met and married in Odessa shortly after the Crimean War, and I was born just ahead of their first anniversary. My father's family had come from the north village, and it was there that my parents returned for my birth. I went to the north village school till I was twelve, and then worked with my parents on the farm. As my twentieth birthday drew nearer, I realized the time had come to find a woman to marry. My mother was eager for grandchildren, and hopeful that the right bride would bring a dowry. We had little land and few friends except through the church, but the girls my age kept to themselves, behind a circle of frowning mothers and aunts who already had plans for their daughters' engagements. None would walk with me or speak to me or even sit in the same pew.

One Sunday I was called to a neighbour's farm to help with a horse that was foaling, and ended up staying well into the night to bring the little fellow into the world. Rather than sleep over, I borrowed a lantern and made my way towards home. It was just a short walk, twenty minutes at most, and I would be in my own bed as the sun rose and so prevent my mother's worry.

Halfway along, I saw what looked like a bundle of rags piled off to one side of the road. I knew to be cautious, as such things could be a trick of thieves or the sign of an animal attack. As I drew closer, I saw that within the rags was a woman, young and pale, close to my age, curled up asleep. I cleared my throat and she sat up, startled, brandishing a tiny knife that could not cut a pear. With some coaxing, she revealed that her name was Magda. She was one of the hill people and had become lost and confused on her way from the village, and then too tired to continue.

Her story was not entirely credible, but she seemed convinced by it, and that was enough. I offered to walk her back towards the hills, and added that we could stop along the way at my parents' house for some potatoes, cabbage, and bread if she could use them. You would think I had offered her rubies and pearls. I snuck into the house while she waited outside and filled a bag for her, and in the bag I also put a proper knife to replace the one she carried. I then walked her to where the hills began their rise beyond our fields, and waved and watched as she began her climb.

The faint warm glow on the horizon meant I would have to hurry to be home before dawn. I turned and was surprised when off in the shadows, under the trees, someone called my name. "Yevgeny," she said. Old and cracked and hoarse. I held my lantern out—and only inches from my face there was another. An old woman, but not a woman, a *nyavka*. A forest witch. I had heard there were such wretches in these woods, but I had never seen one. Few things frightened me when I was young, but the sight of her froze me with fear.

"Do you like the girl?" she asked. "I know she likes you. She would make a lovely wife."

"What do you want with me?" I stammered. "I mean you no harm. I just want to go home to my parents. They will wake up soon and they will be worried."

"Oh well, we wouldn't want them to worry," she said mockingly, and then leaned in so close that I could smell blood on her breath. "I promise, young man, I am not here to hurt you. I will not touch even one hair on your head. I have come to offer you a choice, knowing that you are eager to marry and have found your bride at last."

"What kind of offer? What kind of choice?"

"She is the woman you are meant to love, but the fates are most unkind. In a few short hours, her people will be attacked and killed. There is nothing you can do to stop it, here or there or anywhere. If you go to her now, and profess your love, she will do the same, and when the murderers come, they will find you in each other's arms and you will die together. So romantic!"

"Or?" I asked, now more angry than afraid.

"Or you can go home to your worried parents and your little feather bed. Magda will escape, but you will never see her again. And until your dying day you will not know a lover's touch, and will not put life into another's womb."

"What if I go and do not speak to her? What if I warn her people of the danger?"

"They will not trust you and will not believe you," she shrugged. "You'll die, she'll die, everyone will die. Except for me, I'll be right here. I am always here." She pulled an apple from the pocket of her cloak, bit into it, exposing a glistening worm.

"There is no choice," I said in frustration. "I will go home, and she will live."

"Such a good boy," she said as she chewed. "I have

a tiny present for you." She reached into her other pocket, and took out a gleaming gold coin, the likes of which I'd never seen. "Take this," she said. "Never spend it, never sell it, never show it to anyone. But keep it with you always. It is precious now, but one day it will be worthless, and on that day it will save your life." She pressed the coin into my palm and backed into the shadows and vanished.

That afternoon, my father woke me to tell me that the *Okhrana*, the secret police who were not so secret, had descended on one of the hillside settlements, killed the Hutsuls and burned their homes. He and some of the other men went up to see the smoking ruins, and there he found one of our knives, stained with still-wet blood. He looked at me, and I looked at him, but there was nothing for us to say.

I should also tell you: I fought in the Great War years later, as so many did, in the field army, at the Battle of Sarikamish. I always kept the *nyavka*'s coin with me, inside my sock, where no one ever saw it. My right boot was old and worn, and the coin neatly pressed against a hole in the sole, close to the arch of my foot. As the battle neared its end and I was on patrol, I felt the coin crack inside my sock. I looked down and saw that I had stepped on a pipe mine and that the coin had broken off the trigger, so it failed to explode. I marked the mine with my helmet and then stepped well away from it—took off my boot, and then my sock. The coin was smashed to pieces. Worthless, you might say. But it did indeed save my life.

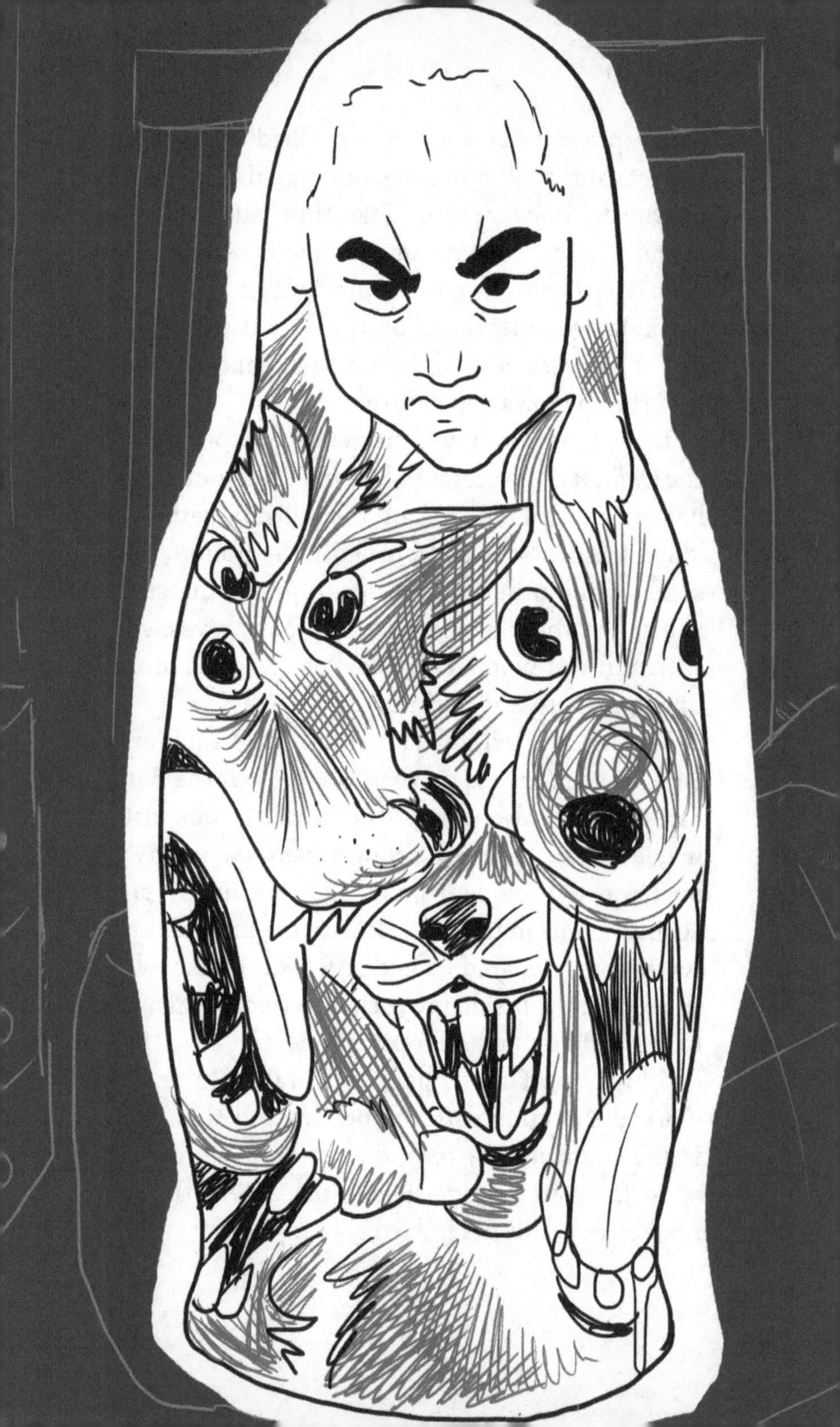

GREGOR

I had been working at the nursing home for nearly three weeks before I saw her. She was one of only a half-dozen residents with a private room and her door was always closed. She had her own nurse, not on staff but from outside, who spoke to no one and answered to no one. Ruta. A large plain woman, brisk and efficient and unknowable. I overheard the nurses at the station near the elevators giggling, calling her Rutabaga, and I glared at them. Ruta arrived at eight each morning and she left at eight each night. I tried the door once shortly after she left for the evening. Locked.

I knocked and asked, "Hello? Are you all right? Is there anything you need?" Silence.

"Leave her alone," the head nurse barked. "She's not our concern. She'll ring if she needs to, she's old but she's capable." I blushed and stammered that I had heard a noise, which was true—it sounded like something had fallen to the floor and was being dragged across it. The head nurse was not interested in what I had heard. She just stood there and glared at me until I gave a short sharp nod, excused myself and hurried away.

Simone, the old woman's chart said. A pretty name, but not her real name, this I knew. Not the name she was born with.

Two days later, Ruta was in the room with Simone, the door shut tight, when a faint metallic chirping could suddenly be heard. The door abruptly opened and Ruta rushed out talking into her cellphone, her voice low and urgent. She left the door wide open and I could see inside. I could see Simone, sitting up in the bed, staring out the window, watching the sunlight filter through the breeze-brushed leaves of the trees beyond. Then she slowly turned her head in my direction and she stared at me. And the corners of her mouth curled into a faint sly smile. My phone buzzed in my pocket. I pulled it out, glanced at the screen. *SOON*, it said. Unknown number. A message from the company.

Ruta hurried back down the hallway, her phone still pressed to her ear, stomped back into Simone's room, and slammed the door shut. Still, I had seen her, aged and frail, alert and amused, and she had seen me.

The following day, just after dawn, the nursing station received a call. Ruta was dealing with a family issue, and the agency had no one available until after the weekend. The others seemed nervous, frightened even, so I volunteered to look in on Simone as part of my rounds.

"No no," the head nurse exclaimed. "This resident is difficult and requires undivided attention. I will distribute your regular duties among the rest of the team." The others nodded, relieved at this decision.

It seemed odd that they would each rather take on another hour of work than tend to a woman who could barely move, who likely could barely speak, who probably ate little and slept for hours on end.

One of them, Carlita, came to me after, in the kitchenette behind the station, and thanked me. "We had a sudden storm one night," she explained, "and I had to go in to shut the window, which was rattling with the wind, keeping everyone awake. I had nightmares for weeks after." Why, I asked, what did she do? What did she say? "Nothing," said the nurse. "She just sat there in the bed, staring and smiling. But the whole time, it was as if cold fingers were being pressed around my throat, I thought I would pass out and fall to the floor. I just couldn't get warm after that, in the middle of the hottest summer. I hope it's better for you, but I couldn't bear to go through it again."

I finished making my cup of tea and went to Simone's room, tapped on the door, unlocked it and entered, closing the door behind me. As before, she was seated on the bed, staring out the window. A grey day today, not much to see.

"Hello," I said. "Your regular nurse is away for a few days. I will be taking her place."

"Good," she said, still looking away. This one word was heavy and hoarse, thickly accented. I recalled my grandfather, pouring me a dram of *medivka* to help me sleep when I was small. "Good," he would say, patting my head. It was one of the few English words that he knew.

"I'm not sure what your regular routine is," I

continued. “There are very few notes in your file. Are you able to tell me how we should spend our days together?”

A few seconds passed and then she spoke, softly and deliberately. “I hear the sound of my home in your voice. It touches your words like smoke.”

I nodded. “My parents were from Ukraine. My father from Grozau, my mother . . .” I let myself trail off. There was no need to go into all that now.

“I know Grozau,” she said, and for a moment I imagined she could see it out the window, across mountains and ocean, snow and trees. “You must tell me a story, with this voice of yours. Something from Grozau, or from your childhood.” And then she turned to look at me as she had that one time before—less like a woman would, more like a doll. Her chest and arms remained still, while her head turned on her neck as if a small child was holding and forcing it. “It need not be true. A fairy tale will suffice. But I do like a good story.” And then she smiled that smile.

And so I did. And as the words came out of my mouth, my whole world fell away.

When I finished that night, just after eight, I put on my coat, walked past the usually chatty and cheery women at the nurse’s station. They kept their distance, murmured to each other as I walked past, averting their eyes. No goodbyes, no goodnights, no see-you-tomorrows. I let the door swing shut behind me, I walked to the centre of the parking lot. I stopped. I lifted my head up, clenched my eyes and my fists, my fingernails digging into my palms, and I screamed and screamed and screamed.

Tell me a story. Something from your childhood.

Across the lot, a light flickered on inside of a sleek black sedan. A man was seated behind the wheel, black overcoat, blood red scarf, black hat shadowing his face with its brim. I could not see his eyes, but I felt his gaze meet mine. I stood very still.

The light snapped off.

As I walked home, I thought about finding a boy. I hadn't had such thoughts in months, the medication was meant to prevent this, but with every block, at every streetlight and bus shelter, with every step, the impulse grew stronger. The last had been three years before. Then, like now, I was new in the city, in for a job, just four weeks, this time in a hospital: a mute old man, a simple injection, no suspicions aroused. The company placed me there, as they had before. A week or two to establish myself, learn the rhythms, find the quiet moments, each placement is different. Then make the kill. Then another few weeks of cart-pushing, sheet-changing, bedpan-dumping, making sure no loose ends, and off to the next.

The night I put the old man down, another good night for a walk, I decided to treat myself. I knew where the boys were, I always know where they are. This one, Danny, twelve at the time, in the back of an unlocked rental car, eyes, tongue, delicious. Pelvis disrupted, intimately damaged. But alive. I never read or watch the news, but oh he was everywhere.

Relieved of the burdens of sight and speech, requiring constant assistance. Thinking of me, my face over his, every time strange fingers and instruments entered his body to construct a new way to shit.

And then, afterwards—four days? Five days? I could scarcely believe it. Transferred to my hospital, onto one of my floors. It was late, dead of night, I was on my last round, I turned a corner with my cart and there he was. Light on above his bed, a light he could feel but that could not pierce his darkness. He was alone, awaiting his morning procedure, and there I was,

at his door,
at his bedside,
leaning in,
he could smell me,
he could feel me,
touching him,
his bird-like chest,
his bandaged face,
leaning in close and whispering,
"I'm still hungry. . . ."

—then him keening and spluttering and thrashing in his bed, while I was back out the door, up the hallway, in a supply room, door locked, pitch dark, gasping, heart racing, cock hard and leaking. I left that night, left that city, so close, nearly caught, so foolish, not tonight, not ever, what was this, what was happening, what was happening to me?

A fairy tale will suffice. It need not be true.

I had decided to humour the old woman with a story that one of my aunts had told me, certain that she would know it as well, The Fox and the Three Hens. But something happened in the telling, it twisted on my tongue so that instead of outwitting the fox and escaping, the birds fell one by one, gutted, consumed, leaving shredded flesh, stripped feathers, heaps of bones in the nests, the impoverished farmer and his wife standing outside in tears.

The old woman laughed heartily, her head bobbing on her neck, while I sat baffled. "But that's not how it's supposed to end," I said, as much to myself as to her. "Is that how it ends?" I looked up at her. Was she laughing at the story, or was she laughing at me?

"I like your version better, I dare say. It has the ring of truth about it. They never could outsmart a fox, and would never work to save each other. They are chickens!" She laughed a little while longer, then said, "Bring your chair over and come sit closer. Take my hand while I sleep a little. My lunch is at noon, my supper at six. You can feed me and then, later, yourself."

I pulled my chair into the space between her bed and the windowed wall, lifted the heavy woollen blankets and crisp white sheets, and clasped her hand in mine. It was tiny, and cold as frost-laced glass, the flesh of the fingers shrivelled against their slender bones. I had not seen her move them, and wondered if she could. I considered doing it then, right that second, I wouldn't even need the injection. There are so many ways to kill someone, especially someone so old. But the company had been clear, the messages explicit: I would have to wait another two days, follow the protocol, then await further instruction.

She might not even live another two days, I thought. What then? And what of Ruta's departure? Was that the work of the company, or might she come back in the morning and take over the old woman's care? What would be so easy now could soon be close to impossible.

Suddenly her fingers stretched against my palm, their tips running the length of my hand to my wrist, circling there, resting there, against my tattoo. She couldn't have seen it, how would she have known? I had kept it well concealed. I looked up to her face, to see through it into her thoughts, but she was already drifting off, her eyes closed, her mouth moving slightly, releasing a breath or a whisper.

"I knew . . ."

I leaned in closer. "Your grandmother, I . . . knew her at the factory. . . ." And then a sigh, and then she was asleep.

A moment later, so was I.

I seldom dream. I sleep like a stone. But as I pitched forward into the darkness, another world opened before me. I emerged in a cold, cavernous room, clapped together out of grey wooden planks, smelling of wet straw and hot sweet blood, and I was smaller, much smaller, and the shrieking—I was a boy, there were three of us, boys, small boys, five or six years old, stripped naked and screaming, and the dark man had come for us—he stood in the doorway with his arm extended, his long sharp silver knife flashing moonlight around us. He seized the youngest of us by the throat, lifted him, and with one swipe gutted him, his insides spilling in a slick black flood onto the dirt floor. The next saw a chance to run through the door but the dark man threw the first aside, grabbed the other in mid-escape, slashed his throat so that his head barely held to his spine, and then brought the blade downward, splitting ribs, slicing innards, filling the room with the stench of bile and waste. In that moment, I looked past the dark man to see my parents, my father and mother—

—but my mother is dead—

—no, just my father, standing, sobbing, whispering the rosary in the old language of his father and of fathers before.

And then the dark man looked up at me, reached for me, lunged for me, and as his face hurtled towards mine—his face—my face—

—and then that sound, something thudding on the floor and dragging across it—

The old woman squeezed my hand and gently shook me awake. "My dear," she said, "I know they say not to wake a man from his nightmares, lest they come true. But you were in quite a state of distress."

"It's . . . all right," I slurred. My tongue was thick, my brain heavy and slow. "This dream has already come true."

"You may want to step into my lavatory," she confided, glancing downward. "You seem to have had an accident."

I pulled the grey vinyl folding door shut behind me. Simone had the only private washroom in the whole facility, and by far the best equipped, with a specially outfitted washbasin, toilet, and walk-in shower-bath. She must have paid for these herself. To one side stood a wardrobe with a selection of uniforms, hanging and folded, in several sizes and colours. "Whose are these?" I called.

"My previous attendants often kept changes of clothing here," she replied. "Everything is clean. If you find something that fits, feel free to wear it."

I changed out of my soiled pants, used the basin and toilet to wipe myself down, then looked through the wardrobe. Only four of the uniforms were for men, with none of the pants the right size, but one pair of white women's slacks—Ruta's, I assumed—fit almost perfectly.

"Much better," Simone said as I re-entered the room. "I am afraid you slept through dinner. It is nearly the end of your shift. I did not want to wake you, you seemed so tired, and peaceful until those last few moments."

While it must have been there all along, I only just then noticed a covered tray on a trolley beside her bed. "I could feed you now, if you like."

"No, no, thank you, I rang for one of the young nurses, she came in and fed me. Somewhat nervous at first, but in the end quite pleasant. Someone will wheel that away later on, nothing left under there but gristle and bones."

I glanced at my watch. It was indeed the end of my shift. As I went to open the door, I remembered—then turned to face her, but she was already watching out the window, into the night. "You said something before you fell asleep. You said you knew my grandmother."

"Did I? I was very tired. When you are my age, sleep sneaks up and takes hold so quickly."

"But, is it true? Did you know her? At the thimble factory?"

"Yes, of course," she said. "I remember her well. So much is lost to me now, but those days will live with me always."

I sat on the bed next to her, took her hand. She still did not look at me. "Then, you must know who I am."

"Yes," she sighed, and faced me at last. "We all do, we knew from the moment you arrived. Who you are and why you are here." Her hand turned mine over, her fingers pushed my sleeve up, exposing the sword and crescent tattoo. "You have come to kill me."

"How do you know I won't kill you now?" I asked.

"Because those are not your orders," she replied, turning my hand over and patting it gently. "Two more days."

I stood up, smoothed the bedclothes. "Very well then," I said as I moved towards the door. "I'll see you in the morning."

"I know you will." She turned her gaze back to the window. "Pleasant dreams." And then the whole of the nightmare rushed into my head, and I vomited on the floor.

And then the coat, the night, the cold. The parking lot. The screaming. The shadowed face in the sleek black car. And the light snaps out.

I'm telling this story in circles, I know. This is all I can do anymore. The words are twisting, tangling on my tongue. Or they would, if I still had a tongue.

That night, after my long walk home and my thoughts of finding a boy, I barely slept, if I slept at all. I tossed from side to side in the hard hotel bed, aching, sweating, teeth chattering, mind racing. Could I have picked up a virus from work? Could it be food poisoning? I thought about going to the hospital, but then a voice like an alarm sounded from the back of my brain: no—no hospital—stay away—it's not safe. I cleared the idea from my mind and lay among the clammy sheets, pulling them up, pushing them down, counting the minutes until the morning light crept into my room. My eyes had just started to close, the darkness about to envelop me, when I was startled awake by my buzzing phone. *ONE MORE DAY*, read the message.

I typed back. *SHE KNOWS EVERYTHING. WHAT DO I DO?*

No response.

It was 8 A.M. I was already late. I peeled back the covers and pulled myself out of the bed.

When I arrived at the nursing home, the main floor station was deserted, the others already on their rounds or in the break room or elsewhere in the building. I went directly into Simone's room, my coat and boots still on—and was surprised to find her bed empty and unmade. I looked over towards her washroom, and there she was, seated in a wheelchair, watching me intently. She wore a blue velour dressing gown, faded and worn, embroidered with flowers around the collar and sleeves. Her hair was down, and long, and steely grey with streaks of white at the temples.

"There you are," she said. "Come, it is time for my bath."

I took off my boots, draped my coat over a chair by the door, and wheeled her into the washroom. I had bathed elderly people before, including my father, who at the end of his life had retreated into a dense dark fog from which he had rarely emerged. I was familiar with withered bodies, hollowed sagging breasts, skeletal arms and legs, shrivelled genitals. But Simone—well, already I had spent more time alone with her, had spoken longer with her, than with all of my previous targets together. The thought of undressing her, touching her, helping her, made me uneasy. She already knew too much about me, and I about her. And despite her fragility, something about her intimidated me, perhaps even frightened me, which was absurd, and irritating in its absurdity.

"Do not be afraid," she said. "I will not bite you."

"Maybe I'll be the one to bite you," I replied, and she laughed.

I wrapped her hair up in a thin white towel, turned on the bath water, let it run till it was just slightly warmer than the inside of my wrist, then pulled the dressing gown away from Simone's body. She was fine-boned and small-jointed, like a ballerina, or a marionette, a web of fine lines over her otherwise taut skin. I felt as if I could hold her in the palm of my hand. I lifted her from the wheelchair onto the stool in the tub, drizzled some soap onto a sponge, dipped it in the warm water, and began to wash her back and neck.

"How many people have you killed?" she asked. "Do not worry, no one can hear us. Your secrets are safe with me."

"I don't know, thirty, forty," I replied. "I don't keep count."

"All for your current employer?"

"No," I said, squeezing a stream of water onto her shoulders. "I was discharged from the armed forces after an accident, then hired as an independent in the Middle East. That did not go as planned, but in the aftermath I was engaged by a contractor in Kiev."

"Spadok," she said. She sensed my surprise to hear the word. "In English, the word is Legacy. They are known by a number of names. They have existed on several continents, for more than two hundred years."

I shrugged. "I know only as much as they tell me. I do what they tell me to do." I added more soap to the sponge and gently washed her chest and belly, her arms and sides.

"You have killed four of us. For Spadok."

"You will be the fifth, yes," I said. "Be careful, the seat is slippery."

She pulled herself back onto the stool while I again rinsed the sponge and filled it with water, let it cascade down the front of her body. "Five of us, all of us old, all of us close to death. Do you know why you are killing us?"

"Something to do with the war, I assume. Something about the thimble factory."

"Yes," she said, "something about that. If you hand me the sponge, I can wash the rest myself." Relieved, I soaped the sponge and handed it to her, and she lightly scrubbed along and between her thighs.

"Any other questions?" I asked. I sounded more impatient than I had intended, and immediately regretted it. I had no one to talk to about my work for Spadok, or about the events that had led me to join them. She had asked, and she had listened. I knew I had crossed a line from my very first answer, but it felt like a line that I needed to cross.

"The water is cold now," I added, "and I should see to your lunch."

"Thank you," she said. "I appreciate your honesty. I knew this day would come eventually. You are very kind to humour an old woman."

I pulled a towel from the rack and placed it around her shoulders, helped her dry herself, and then wrapped her in the dressing gown. I wheeled her back to her bed and helped her into it. The bath had refreshed her, brought some colour back into her cheeks, but it had exhausted me. "You look so unwell," she said. "Why don't you sit down and close your eyes for a moment. Lunch will be here soon, and then we can have story time."

I sat in the bedside chair and again my eyelids descended as if under they were under a spell. I heard someone singing—Simone? I couldn't be sure. A lullaby from the first land, ancient even in the time of the Tsars. The words and the tune were familiar but I couldn't think why or from where. I felt a warmth all around me, as if I was drifting in spring water, gentle hands cradling my head and neck, lovingly guiding me out into the middle of a midnight lake under a sky full of stars. And then the hands, so many hands, reached up from under the water's surface, and clutched at me and pulled me under.

I awoke to the sound of a scream, and the scream was my own.

"Oh, I am sorry, I startled you," Simone said, setting the metal cover down over her lunch tray. "I was trying to be quiet. I have just finished my meal—but I asked for some soup for you and the nurse very kindly obliged." I looked and saw there was a second tray closer to me, at the foot of the bed, with a steaming bowl of broth and dumplings. The trolley was parked along the wall by the door.

"I think she was worried about you," the old woman added. "I told her you were fighting something off."

"I'm not sure that I'm hungry," I sighed. I still felt oddly queasy. Perhaps it was a virus after all.

"Please, for me." She held out the spoon. "You must keep up your strength. Tomorrow will be a difficult day."

I reluctantly took the spoon, and sipped a bit of the broth. It was salty and earthy and smoky, and its nourishment seemed to go from my mouth to my throat to my stomach into my veins. I raised one of the dumplings to my lips, and took a bite: *varenyky* filled with what seemed to be pork and green onion. I chewed slowly and let the flavour flow over my palate, then looked down and saw, just for a moment, a half-eaten eyeball perched on my spoon and I gasped and dropped it onto the tray with a clatter.

"Be careful, my dear," Simone said, reaching over to hand me a napkin. "You would not want to burn yourself."

I finished the rest of the dumplings and broth, and went to place my tray on the trolley. I looked over and saw that the iron grate on the floor had been moved, leaving a large square hole in the floor. "Someone from the building came in earlier. Looking for mice. I have never seen a mouse in all my years here, and I told them so, but still."

I nodded, went to pick up the grate but it was too heavy to lift, so I dragged it across the floor and pushed it into place with a thump. I could see from the marks in the wood that it had been moved many times before, though obviously not by Simone. Once or twice a year, I surmised, to put down poison or traps.

"Now it is my turn to tell you a story," she said, "one you may know from your childhood. It was told to me by my mother, and I am sure that mothers still tell in the town where I was born." She must have seen me shift in my seat, for she reached over and gave my cheek a squeeze. "Do not worry, it is short, and after I have finished you can go home to rest. I have already arranged for dinner alone." I nodded and sat up in my seat, and she collected her thoughts and began.

"In a neighbouring village, when I was a child, there was a girl somewhat younger than me—we will call her Rosina. She was a good girl, obedient and helpful, but she was a solitary soul and would sometimes go off by herself in the barn or the fields or in a small grove of trees halfway to town. One day, her mother called her in for supper but she didn't come in. Her father called and called, and went to the barn and searched through the fields but he could not find her. Dusk had turned to darkness, so the mother and father dressed in their warmest clothes and brought their brightest lanterns, and an old dog they once used for hunting but now was nearly blind and deaf, and went to the grove of trees hoping to find Rosina there."

I felt another shudder of nausea. This story was oddly familiar, but something about it was inside-out, or wrong-way-round. Where had I heard it? Who would have told me?

"As they came closer to the grove, the dog began to bark and bark, so the father left the mother standing with the dog while he went to investigate. And there he found his daughter, Rosina—she had been attacked by a beast and nearly torn to shreds but, even though hours had passed, she was somehow still alive. He bundled her up in his coat and ran to his wife and together they hurried back to their house.

They cleaned and dressed her wounds and cooled her burning fever, all while the old dog continued to bark and howl outside. They took turns staying with her through the night, and by morning Rosina was nearly healed, her wounds and scratches almost gone. The mother and father decided not to tell anyone what had happened, as they did not understand it themselves. From then until her wedding day, and until she and her husband had a daughter of their own, Rosina was always healthy and happy, and the dog never came back inside the house. It lived out its days in the barn and died there at a ripe old age."

The nausea was coming in waves now, but I couldn't move, I couldn't stop listening, I had heard this story, I knew this story, but I still did not know how or why.

"The day after Rosina's daughter was born, an old woman from the village came to the farm to visit. Rosina's father had long since died but her mother was still alive. The old woman was a healer, and sent Rosina's husband off to pick mushrooms so that she could speak to the two women alone.

And when they were alone, she said: "Many years ago, Rosina, you were attacked in the grove by a beast. Ever since that day, you have carried the blood of the beast within you, and you have passed that blood to your daughter. You must watch her as she grows, for if that beast emerges, your daughter will have to be killed. As will her children."

"Strigoi," I whispered. "The beast was a *strigoi*."

"Yes," Simone said gravely.

"Rosina was my grandmother—and her daughter was my mother."

"Yes. And that is why your mother was killed. And your brothers as well. You should have died too. But somehow, you survived."

I tried to stand, tried to push myself out of the chair, but instead I collapsed to the floor, onto my knees and then on my side. "Am I also—a beast?" I gasped.

"You have the blood. You have your urges. Then again, you might just be an ordinary monster." She knelt down, pulled a blanket from the foot of her bed over me as I lay clenched and shivering. "Yes, Ruta and I, we know quite a bit about you. You see, we are the ones who contracted you, through Spadok. We are the ones who arranged your assignments. The four men you killed, they were the last of your grandmother's torturers."

The door opened, and a familiar pair of heavy white shoes entered the room, stepped around and behind me. Two strong arms lifted me up. I tried to writhe, to squirm and struggle, but I was paralyzed. The arms dropped me, a dead weight, onto the bed by Simone's feet. I looked up and saw Ruta standing over me, holding her cellphone close to my face. *SOON*, said her message to me.

"I knew Rosina, in the thimble factory, and I saw what happened to her," Simone continued. "Just before the war, the Russians used the factory to conduct experiments of a hideous nature. Your grandmother, who carried the beast blood, she suffered greatly there. She was still just a child. We helped her escape, and kept her hidden, and in time her gifts revealed themselves."

"Her . . . gifts?" I asked weakly. Suddenly I heard the familiar sound, of something being dragged across the floor, and I realized: it was the heavy iron grate. I turned my head slightly, and watched as one dark hairy hand, and another, and another, grasped the edge of the bed. Then more hands, more arms, reaching up and over, reaching for me. And then face, and eyes, and teeth, and tongue.

"Oh, look, here she is," Simone said with a smile. "She looks excited to see you."

The face loomed closer, and then somehow blurred and bloomed. Eyes and more eyes, mouth upon mouth, hands on my cheeks, in my hair, on my chest. "How many . . . are there?" I asked. "What else . . . is here?"

"No one else, nothing else," Simone replied. "Just her." And with that, two of the hands pried open my jaw, and another grabbed hold of my tongue. And then one of the mouths pressed onto my eye, and she said, "I think she must be hungry."

It is dark down here, I think, down here where my grandmother lives. Thin ribbons of light shine down from the grate, from cracks between the boards. I turn my head and see the shapes of others, slumped against the walls, some alive, some not. She feeds on both. She feeds on me. A finger here, a toe there. Sometimes more.

I'm telling this in circles, I know. Inside-out and wrong-way-round. The words are twisting, tangling. I sleep, I wake, I watch the ribbons of light, I wait.

I have the blood of the beast in me. Maybe I do not know how to die. Waiting is all I can do.

But:

We have some time, before she comes. An hour or two perhaps. Tell me a tale, something from your childhood. I do like a good story.

TWO
THE NIGHT POLICE

SABINA

There was a time in the history of our three neighbouring villages when very few children were being born, and almost no girls. *Movchanya.* This period lasted nearly ten years. Even today, no one knows why, though of course there are theories—some to do with the factory, some with the government, some to do with the land on which our villages were built, and a few blaming our own tainted bloodlines.

We do not speak of it now, but at the time it was quite traumatic. Many women struggled to become pregnant but, of the few that succeeded, most of them miscarried within the first two months. Nearly a dozen women carried their babies into the ninth month but the children were either stillborn or so severely deformed that they could barely take a breath. Some men left the villages for the city, married there and brought their wives back, but it did not matter. The results were the same. In those ten years, among our villages, only thirty children lived. Only six of them girls.

I came in the seventh year. I was born a boy but was raised as a girl. Of course I did not understand this at the time, and I do not know now whether I was drawn to girlish things before my parents chose this, or because they chose it. But what's done is done. I was not the only such child—four others were also raised this way, three older than me and one younger—but I was the only one from my village. Our parents ensured, as we grew, that we always wore something green: a dress or skirt, or a ribbon, or a wristlet or stockings, to set us apart from the others. We were known as the *Zeleni Divuski*, the Green Girls.

There was some teasing, naturally, as we grew up, and there was some fear. We were treated differently, some felt "specially," and that is always difficult for children. In time, though, the girls outside our group, even the older ones, would come and tell us their secrets, and the boys would come and ask us how to make the girls like them.

The boys would often practice with us—not sexually, of course, but with holding hands and talking and kissing. "Too rough, too fast," we might say to one. "Too shy, too quiet," to another. We encouraged boys to ask questions and to listen, to be less boastful, to be more polite and considerate. "Is this how you talk to your mother?" we would ask. Once a boy answered, "I don't have a mother," and one of us too quickly said, "I don't doubt it." We tried not to make the boys cry, but there were times.

And then we would report back to the girls about who was funny and charming, who was strong and shy, who was quick and boisterous. They all wanted to know who kissed best but we would not tell them. "Find out for yourselves!" we would laugh. It was all harmless fun, and some good matches and good families resulted from our encouragements. Though it wasn't till many years later that we found understanding wives, or husbands, for ourselves.

This was all well before the war. The villages were situated on lands in constant dispute—not only between countries but among landowners, religions, and even species. There were stories of the *Drevniye*, the beings who came before all of us, and how some lived alongside us in peace and even sheltered with us to disguise their presence. We had heard talk of the shapeshifters but never knew if they lived among us or whom they might be. And there were dark tales of the *Naystarsha*, who lived deep beneath the ground and who was the source of all the *Drevniye* power. Fairy stories, all of them, but still.

One day, when I was seventeen, a summer day I think, or very early in the fall, I was sipping some tea in the square when a much younger girl came over to me and said, "You should think of leaving this place. All the Green Girls. And soon."

I was shocked that someone so young should be so bold. "Why do you say this to me?" I asked. "Who are you? And why should I leave?" She held her finger to her lip, and then whispered. "Meet with the others, tonight if you can." She peered into my eye. "Your mother has a sister in Satu Mare. Go to her. If you need to travel farther, you will know." Then she looked around, and I looked around, and saw that a few of the villagers were standing a respectful distance away, watching us. I thought I knew everyone in the village, but now I was surrounded by strangers.

"How long do we have?" I asked. "How long must we be gone?"

"Tomorrow at noon should still be safe. But tonight is better. Take everything you love."

Something in those last few words chilled me deeply. I curtsied to her, to all of them, and turned, and hurried home. I told my mother her sister was ill, a mutual friend in town had said so, and that we must see her at once. She bundled my father and our dog into the cart with some clothing and provisions, and we were off just after dinner. I made us stop at the other villages, told the other Green Girls the story. Three were able to join us. Little Maruska was ill with a terrible cough and couldn't be moved, so I urged her parents to follow as soon as they could. I then apologized to my mother for the now-obvious lie, but she could see how frightened I was, how frightened we all were and, well, if it was a trick, a prank of some sort, we'd at least have taken a trip together and oh how surprised my aunt would be.

Little Maruska never did join us. And we never went back. We heard in the end what happened, of course. I still do not know why we were saved.

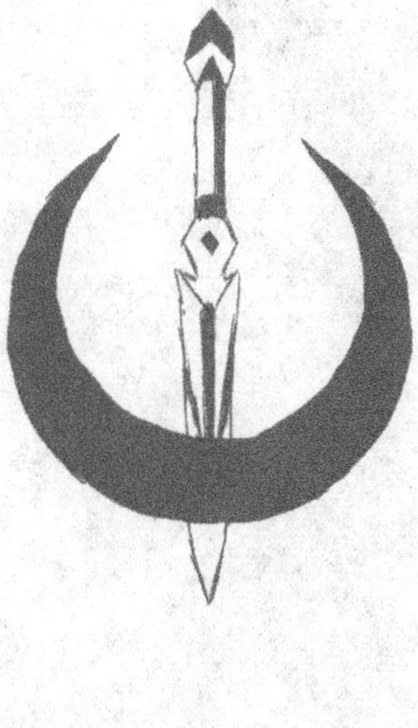

MARIUS

If you feel something strike you on the shoulder or leg or on your side, as if someone has slapped or punched you, and no one is near who could have done so, fall down.

I did so. My brother did not. He was hit three more times and died. I stayed on the ground until I heard shouts and shots and men running up, farmers and villagers, neighbours, and only then did I dare stir.

I lost so much blood, and yet I lived.

My mother had told us a war was coming, said it was not far from us and inching closer day by day. She never spoke to anyone, never left our house, and yet she knew this. Now it was on our doorstep.

Hunters had come from time to time, before I was born, in twos and threes. Ours was an old village, and the oldest among us had fled from other old villages, and their parents and grandparents from other old villages before. We heard stories of special officers, police who were more like soldiers, whose task it was to rid the world of our kind. Our village had been a sanctuary, but now it was a trap.

Sacha's father Yuri found the hunters in the

woods, where they had been cornered by some of the whispering folk upon whom their weapons were useless. Half-mad, they had curled up and torn at themselves, crying and shrieking at what they had heard. Yuri and other men from the village tied the hunters and led them to the church for questioning before the congregation. It took hours before they died—but in his last breath, the older one confessed to a number: five hundred.

"That one," my mother said. "What he says is true. I see them. Five hundred coming. They will be here before dawn."

Yuri slit the older man's throat and threw his body to the ground. The last trickles of blood meandered towards the drain in front of the altar, where the *Naystarsha* hid beneath, the warm red droplets moistening her tangle of tongues. "What can we do?" Yuri hissed. "We cannot fight five hundred. We cannot run."

"Some can run," my mother said. "Some can hide, for a time. What we cannot do is stay and wait. Here, they will kill us all." She turned to the gathered villagers. The room was nearly full; I had never seen her speak to so many at once.

"You who are descendants of the Northern Families, you must go to the forest. Take nothing with you. The woods have paths and protections. You who came to us from the Eastern Edge, you will be safest close to the water. Travel past the lake and along the rivers. Your children know a network of caves that you have never seen. Trust them, and they will lead you. We who are oldest and weakest, we must feed the *Naystarsha*, so that she may survive in solitude until this darkness passes. The rest must fight, to help to save the others."

"What of the factory?" someone asked from the back of the room.

"The factory is already gone," my mother said. "Everyone there is gone." There were gasps in the room, and murmurs, and sobs. But it was as if we already knew.

"What you describe is hopeless," Yuri said. "We must stay together, we must band together and fight!"

"Yuri," she said kindly, "you are a good man and a strong man, but you are not the one to lead us. Take my hand."

Confused, he took her hand and she held him gently. His eyes began to cloud over, he grew pale and frightened. "What is happening?" he whispered. "Why can't I see? Why can't I speak?"

"Shhhh," she said calmly, "you are having a dream, that is all, an odd, confusing dream." She gestured to me to pull the altar grate from the floor. I did so, and felt the coarse bristly tongues of the *Naystarsha* brush against my fingers. "You will wake up soon, and the world will be bright and new and full of joy," and she led him to the drain and dropped him in. The tongues whirled around him like razors. He didn't even scream.

"Now, all of you," she said to the room. "You know what to do, and you must do it now. There is no time." Just then, gunshots began to ring out from the most distant fields. Dozens and dozens of villagers filed out, and seven more—old, infirm, injured—came to the front.

My mother took the hand of the first—"You will feel no pain"—and led him over the drain where the tongues welcomed him. She took another's hand—"You will feel no pain"—and again, and again, until all who were with us had been consumed. She turned to me.

"Why don't you stay?" I asked. "You can run or hide. You know much more than they do."

"I will only hold them back. What they need to know to survive, they will learn in the coming days."

"Is it true? Will we wake up in a world that's bright and new and full of joy?"

"No," she said. "Our heaven, such as it was, was here. We lived, we loved, we saw beautiful and terrible things, and now it ends." She stepped forward, clutching me. "You will feel no pain," she whispered—and together we fell into the abyss.

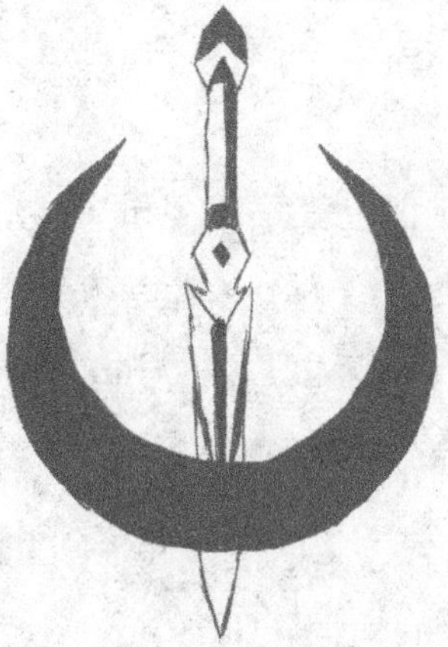

ELENA

Shortly after we were married, my husband Antoniu and I left our village and travelled south—first to Odessa and then to Izmail on the banks of the Danube. His family had a history there, as he was of Wallachian blood, but his last ancestors had been driven from the area more than a century before.

Once we arrived, I discreetly set up shop in our basement rooms as a fortune teller. Such activities were prohibited in the days leading up to the war, and violence was on the rise. However, the wealthy and powerful craved knowledge of their futures, and soon my clientele grew to include the wives of the mayor and the chief of police. What no one knew was that my husband had the true gift, and that I was merely his mouthpiece. While watching from a nearby chair or listening from behind a curtain, Antoniu would send his voice into my head with his observations and predictions and I would repeat them, eliciting gasps.

Much of what troubled these women was mundane. "I see you are considering an affair," I would say to one, and to another I would note, "Your husband has a wandering eye." To a third I would ask, "Have you checked your jewellery box lately? Some pieces may be missing," and to another, "Are you prepared to have another child? Because it seems that you are carrying one." Tears of gratitude were not unusual, accompanied by generous gifts to increase good luck and ward off the Evil Eye.

As the war grew closer, though, the women changed as their husbands changed, and so did the questions they brought to me. "Will my son be called into battle?" asked one. "Is my neighbour a spy?" asked another. "Are we safe? Should we flee? What cities, what countries, will be spared?" The answers were difficult, as the decisions of a few remote men changed the futures of millions day by day. The women became more desperate, bringing gold and jewels and other valuables to pay for their sittings—and then abruptly they stopped coming. The streets were tense and still. Even the birds were afraid to fly.

The third evening, after supper, Antoniu brought out an old leather bag, and filled it with nearly all we had earned, tied it tight with twine and handed it to me. "Put on my pants and coat and boots," he said, "and keep to the shadows. Go to the cathedral—behind it you will find a stone stairwell that leads down to an ancient cistern. You may enter it tonight, and then again in five years. Hide the bag in the shallow water away from the entrance, at the base of a pillar where you know you will find it."

"Why are you saying this?" I asked. "What is happening?"

"Go now, and do not hurry back," he said, wrapping

his black cloth coat around me. "I am expecting guests." He pressed his hand to my belly, then kissed me on the forehead. "Remember always, Elena, I am never very far from you."

I stepped out the door and into the night, and saw that the military had taken to the streets, as had the police and another force whose insignia was unfamiliar. They knew exactly who they wanted. They went to certain houses and buildings, pulled certain people out into the streets—even the elderly, even children and babies—pushed them onto the ground and shot them.

I ran.

I reached the cathedral and found the stone stairwell, the old wooden door, the passage into the cistern. I paused at a column carved with the visage of Medusa, knelt down and tucked the leather bag into the water beneath it. "We are the children of monsters and of gods," we were always told in the village. It was a comfort to find one here. I kissed her—I do not know why—and then curled up and slept on the floor beneath her unblinking gaze.

Hours later, I crept up the stairs to find that the sun was just starting to rise. The streets were empty and silent. I slipped through the shaded alleys as if led by a cautious child, and as I approached our street, our home—

—I saw my Antoniu being carried out, a bloodied sack over his head. He had been shot. The officer carrying him tossed his body into the back of a military truck, one of several such trucks into which dozens of other bodies had been flung. Those same officers, that same insignia—I know now it was the *Nichni Politsiyi*. Among them, curiously, was our own police chief. He looked up and down the street, then closed our door behind him, stepped into a long oil-black car, and pulled away, followed one-two-three by the corpse-bearing trucks. As the convoy departed, I composed myself and moved back into the alley, found my way to our home's back entrance, ducked back inside and then sobbed until finally I slept.

At noon I awoke, startled by a tapping at the door. I pulled a dressing gown around myself and peered out to see the police chief's wife standing nervously. I ushered her in, sat her down at the table. "My husband was killed last night," I told her. "I expect they meant to kill me, and it's likely they still mean to do so."

"If it comes to that," she replied, "I will protect you. You have great value to us, and to our families. But we could not be seen as favouring your household. A sacrifice had to be made."

I nodded, for what was there to say. "Why have you come?" I asked.

She reached up, unfastened her necklace, placed it on the table between us. "What can I do to live through this war? I don't care about my husband."

Just then, I heard Antoniu as I always had, a whisper high in the back of my head. *"She will not live. She will be dead within the week, whatever she does."*

"It is good you don't care about your husband," I told her. "For he has found a younger woman and is planning to desert you. If you want to live, you must kill him. Tonight."

Tears welled in her eyes. "You see this? This is true?"

Antoniu fell silent within me. "Yes," I said, "it's all so clear. A knife in the neck from behind—be swift and silent." I took her hand in mine. "It is just as you said: a sacrifice has to be made."

She nodded, withdrew her hand, walked out the door and up the stairs. I never saw her again.

BOGDAN

I was the first to be killed when they came onto the factory floor. Normally, when I am at my station, I am farthest from the door, but at this time I was closest because someone had fallen in the change room, or so I was told, and I was the first aid attendant for the morning shift. I have wondered since if someone inside the factory assisted the attack, as I could not see anyone injured when I approached the change room, and then the outside door pulled open abruptly and the gunshots began.

I was struck in the chest and face and fell quickly. Within moments, I felt myself lift up and out of my body, held only by a thin thread of light, and then I was high up near the ceiling, looking down at my bloodied remains and then at the carnage unfolding in the rest of the room.

There were, I think, seven of them in our building, all in dark grey trench coats with black fur collars and black leather caps that were not of the police nor of the military, but from something worse. Two of them sprayed the room with machine guns. The others had semi-automatic pistols that they used to finish anyone still breathing after the hail of bullets.

After just two minutes, thirty of us lay dying, and after six minutes, we were dead. As the machine guns swept one room, then entered and swept another, mechanically, from room to room to room, you could hear the gunfire echo everywhere. And after the shots, the fires were set. In the brief silences in our building, you could hear the *tra-ta-ta* in the other buildings, the rush and roar of hungry flames.

Fifteen minutes, and all were dead. Two hundred and twenty of us. Four escaped, including the girl, and perhaps also the collaborator.

After a time, I felt the thread of light between myself and my body fade and I rose up higher through the floors until I was well above the factory buildings. They were consumed in an immense and terrifying conflagration which could only leave ruins and ash. Every building was burning, even animals and birds were dead. So much was lost that day.

I found in time that I could move of my own accord and that I was undisturbed by wind and smoke, and so I returned to earth and glided to the small cemetery outside the factory gates. I had always found it peaceful and contemplative, and had sometimes wished that I would die during my requirement so that I could be buried there. I settled under a tree, much as I would have if I had been alive, and turned my attention away from the factory buildings towards the three villages and the land beyond.

After what felt like an hour or two—for time was already behaving strangely—a young woman drifted along the road and up over the hillock and came to rest next to me. She said nothing, so I spoke first.

"I thought I was all alone," I told her. "I thought I missed my chance. Hundreds died, in the factory, but I'm the only one I've seen. Except for now, for you. Have the others moved on, to another place? Is that what was meant for us?"

She paused for a moment. "I'm new myself but—I think what happens is you float up and up and, if you don't stop yourself, then you disperse like a mist. You just cease to be. But if you will yourself down, back down to the ground, then this is where you'll stay. I don't know if it's true for everyone, but I'm here and I think that's why."

"What happened to you?" I asked.

She shifted uncomfortably. I almost said that she didn't have to tell me. And then she knelt down beside me, and stared at the ground between us. "I was at home, waiting for my brother to come in from the pasture, when I heard the shots. I looked out, I saw him die, I saw his face. And then the men, two men, they were coming to the house. I had no escape. They grabbed me, held me down, they—violated me, slashed me open. I died. And when I pulled away from my body, I left the house, I looked for my brother. I found his body, but he wasn't there. I looked back at the house and then thought I should go, but didn't know where. I saw the smoke from the factory, so I followed it here, and then I found you."

"Were you angry?" I asked. "Or sad?"

"I was sad," she admitted, "but as I left the farm and started on the road, my sadness began to fade. I knew the thing I feared the most had happened, so I was no longer afraid. It's not peace, exactly, it's more like a stillness." She turned and for the first time met my eyes. "Is it like that for you?"

"I think so," I answered. "I thought I would be lonely. I was always lonely before. But I sat and watched the grass wave in the wind, the sunlight stream through the leaves on the trees. I remembered songs my father played on accordion and violin, I sang them to myself. Yet those things that happened just a few hours ago feel as distant as my grandfather's schoolyard stories. I wonder if we will stay like this, or if something more will happen."

We sat in silence, and then she stood. "I should go," she said. "To my mother's house. My brother might have gone there, it's where we always felt safest." She leaned down, lightly kissed my forehead. "Remember me, if you can."

"I will try," I replied. I watched as she drifted back over the hillock and down alongside the road, and when I looked again she had vanished.

And suddenly it was dusk, and the shadows cast by the setting sun crept past me and up onto the factory wall. My thoughts turned once more to my father, and I began to sing.

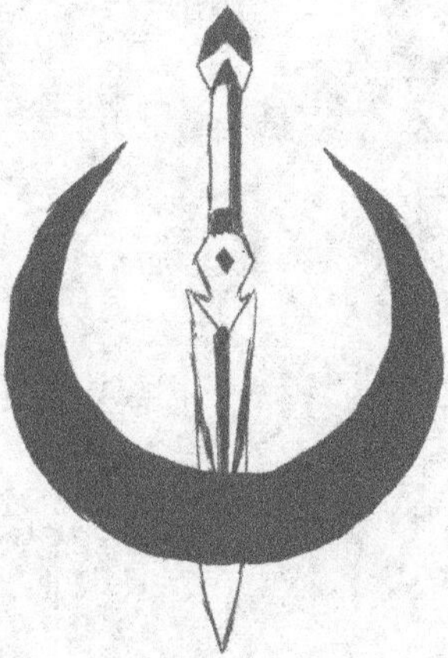

HORIA

Less than a week after my birth, just hours after my mother died, I was adopted by the Grazyns: Maxim, owner of the Grazyn Porcelain Factory and benefactor of the three nearby villages, and his devoted wife Anychka. I never knew who my mother was or where she came from. The Grazyns felt this was best, as my mother had no living relatives and my birth father was unknown. They could not have children themselves, so my early life in many ways was like a fairy story—filled with love and riches and luxury, and loneliness. A feeling that nothing I had belonged to me, and that I in turn belonged to nothing and to no one.

From a young age, I had a tutor, Miss Irina, who was from our region but had been raised in Prague and had travelled through Europe with her family. Twenty years older than me, she was beautiful, if somewhat severe in appearance, and I adored her. She taught me all of the conventional subjects—mathematics, science, history, geography—as well as reading and writing in Russian, German, French, and English. And also embroidery. Mother believed that I should be seen on occasion with a silver needle, a lock of thread, a square of white cotton and a Grazyn thimble on my finger. As it turned out, I had an aptitude for needlework and by adolescence was creating my own elaborate, intricate designs that decorated my bedroom, the family sitting room, the factory chapel, the bereavement suite, and the altars of the churches in the three villages.

In private, I more often used a goat leather thimble, as they were inexpensive and easy to replace, but I appreciated the beauty and the practicality of the porcelain thimble. Smooth and resilient, the Grazyn thimble was unique among porcelain thimbles as the surface was three-quarters painted with delicate motifs, and one-quarter plain. The plain surface, which protected the pad of the finger, was lightly pocked with small indentations to keep the needle from sliding off. As I grew older, these indentations proved delightfully practical for other, less girlish activities—sparking countless fantasies of Miss Irina lifting her bedcovers and welcoming me into her embrace, warming me with her moist red mouth.

I was rarely allowed to interact with other children, and seldom with adults, so for many years Miss Irina was my only friend. She had never married, and never would, but was mindful of the possibility that her caregiving duties might end once a suitable husband was found for me. To their credit, the Grazyns did not impose their will upon me. They concentrated instead on preparing me to run the factory when the inevitable moment came.

It was then, as I turned nineteen, that my father revealed the factory's many secrets, those of the

Grazyns and of the villages around us. His trust in me was implicit, and his calm persistence in the face of my disbelief was itself a powerful demonstration of his faith in me. Yet my image of him, of our family, of our world together was deeply shaken. I wanted to be the good daughter, the capable heir, but I also wanted to run, to escape the ghoulish prison that my fairy-tale palace had suddenly become. And the tiniest part of me, like a shard of ice in my heart, wanted to kill him.

He was a vivisectionist, performing horrific experiments on the living. He was a murderer, a killer even of children. He was a resurrectionist, a body-snatcher. Our wealth, our renown, were founded on decades of his unspeakable acts, and on two hundred years of unspeakable acts by Grazyns before.

And yet, he was my father.

And then a thought, a fine thin blade of dread, ran from the crown of my head down the back of my skull and all the way down my spine. "What of my mother?" I asked. "Was she one of your victims?"

"You are in fact my child," he said softly, "and I am your father. Your mother is Miss Irina."

He leaned closer. "And you are my greatest gift. For while I am human, Irina has the *Drevniye* blood, a sister to the *Naystarsha*. This is why we have kept you from other children, from other people. You are not like them." He reached behind me, under my capelet, unbuckled the leather flap that concealed my other mouths, that held my myriad knife-sharp tongues all snug against my back. He caressed them gently.

"You are the last great hope of Irina's kind, and the crowning achievement of mine. You are the one that lived."

Just then, from below, on the factory floor: shouts and shots and screams, and silence. And then more cries, the smell of smoke, the stink of burning flesh. I turned to him. "What is this? What do we do?"

"The *Nichni Politsiyi*," he said, hushing his voice to a whisper. "Run to the back of the building, to the library, and out through the window. And then to the trees." It was true, the factory backed onto a dense dark forest. Its floor was knotted with roots and vines and nettles but its trees stretched out serenely above the tangle with branches supple and strong. I took his hand to pull him with me but he shook it away. "You cannot lift me, and I cannot climb. I will face them here. Now go." Already footsteps were rushing towards the doors. I turned and ran.

Our rooms were a maze of doors and passages which had been a boon for childhood games of hide-and-seek with Miss Irina, and here I was again, ducking and dodging and peering and scuttling, my heart in my throat as—*tra-ta-ta!*—the gunfire rang out behind me. Father was dead, I knew this, but it was all that I knew. From study to bedroom to hallway to gallery to library I ran, and then stopped. At the window leading out to the forest was Miss Irina. Bleeding. She had been shot, very possibly with silver.

"There is no time," she said. She held her arms out weakly.

I raced to her, enfolded her, pulled her up to the sill

and into the lush leaves above. "You have carried me, and have always carried me, and without a word," I told her. "Now it is my turn."

The doors behind us burst open—but we were already gone.

IVAN

"What I don't get is, why aren't there *more* ghosts?"

"Don't turn here, it's a one-way going north," I said. "You have to go down to the end of this block, take a right, and then go up the next street."

"I mean," he continued, "thousands of people die every day. Terrible deaths, some of them, murders and worse. So what I want to know is," and with this he turned and looked at me, "why aren't we overrun with ghosts? And why are they all from the last few hundred years?"

"There's a ghost in the Bible, in the first book of Samuel. England has a Roman soldier haunting the Essex coast. And Pausanius wrote about one in Ancient Greece, at the site of the Battle of Marathon. I'm sure there's a phantom caveman somewhere."

"What's that, three? Four?" he said, glancing over at me again. "Where are all the others?"

Just keep your eyes on the road," I replied. "I don't care if there are dozens or millions, I'd rather we didn't join them."

He took a pair of flat-fold dust masks out of his pocket,

handed one to me, slipped the other one on himself over his mouth and nose. I tucked mine inside my jacket. He shrugged, pulled out a key on a blue plastic tab, slid it into the lock, wrestled with it until the bolt slid free. He grabbed the knob, pushed the door open. A musty grey cloud floated out to greet us. He gestured for me to enter first. I fanned at the air with my hand, peered into the darkness, stepped inside.

"Just a reminder, I don't clear houses," I said. "It's not my skill set."

"Yes, I know," he answered. "I just want to know what's in here, whether we should even try to reopen it."

Edward House, a brooding pile of crimson brick down in the entertainment district, had been a speakeasy in the '20s, a men's shelter in the '30s, and a mob-connected steakhouse in the '50s. It achieved its true notoriety in the early 1970s as a gay men's bathhouse, with a trend-setting nightclub and lounge that hosted rising disco stars and fading Broadway divas. Grace Jones had played one of her first shows here, and Ethel Merman one of her last. The Edward Baths thrived through *Charlie's Angels*, *Dallas* and *Dynasty*, and then struggled through the early years of AIDS as the illness tore through the city's gay community.

Then, in 1997, there was first a suspicious death, and a few months later a fire that trapped a dozen men on the top floor. Some of them burned to death, some suffocated, and one broke his neck when he leapt from the third-floor window to the pavement below. Police, fire, and ambulance took a leisurely twenty-seven minutes to arrive. Much of the back half of the house was destroyed but the front remained largely intact.

Edward House sat empty for the better part of a decade before Stefan inherited it and began to explore turning it into an event space, suitable for weddings, parties, conferences, and recitals. In the meantime, the building was declared a heritage property, so he spent another five years carefully dismantling the ruined section of the house and developing a plan to rebuild and expand the space within the rigorous and convoluted heritage guidelines. However, something had recently happened with his contractor—one of his crew had ended up in the hospital and the rest had flat-out quit. And that's when Stefan called me.

He reached over to the left of the front door and flicked a switch. A trio of worklights on yellow stands burst on, flooding the area with cool clean whiteness. We were in a large open entryway with a wooden cash desk built into the corner at our immediate left, a pair of solid red oak doors just beyond, and an open archway to the right with another stand of lights just inside waiting to be powered up. A large red oak staircase rose up ahead of us, with a tin sign nailed on the wall at the first step: *No Alcohol Beyond This Point*. On the floor in front of us were some scuffs and gouges where a pair of turnstiles should have been—torn out by the renovator, I supposed, to make it easier to bring large or heavy items in and out the front door. The floors were surprisingly clean, swept maybe two or three days before.

I heard, then felt, a very faint hum that seemed to emanate from within the walls: residual spirits—the most common kind. Remnants of souls, frozen in time, gradually fading over the passing decades. In a warm inviting home they loved in life, their gentle presence can help to create an atmosphere of quiet contentment. Here, there was an edge of despair, confusion, even fear. A chord struck from clashing notes. Not dire enough to cause Stefan any trouble, though, or alarm his future customers. It might even be helpful, encouraging patrons to eat quickly, drink more and leave sooner. I tuned in to the dissonance, filtering out the noise and focusing on the essence. I reached out, touched the wall to my immediate right. A little ripple, like a droplet of ice water, ran from my fingertips up my arm and through my shoulders and chest. Again, not enough to be concerned about, but startling all the same.

Stefan saw my face and frowned. I tried to pull my features back into a more neutral expression. "There are a few things going on here. It will take me a while to sort them out. Are all the doors unlocked?"

"Everything but the basement," he answered. "I can let you in there now if you like."

"No no, it's fine. I think most of what I'm looking for is on the upper floors."

I looked through the arch on the right into the large empty room, the bordello red paint on the walls cracking and peeling to reveal the old white calcimine underneath. More must, more damp, with an edge of smoke and rot. Risers in front of the bay window suggested a platform for a DJ booth or a tiny stage, aptly placed in front of the modest wooden dance floor in the centre of the room. In the darkness at the back I could make out the generous curve of a bar with rows of empty liquor shelves behind. Plastic sheeting and some yellow caution tape sealed the room off from those at the back of the house. The hum was stronger here, richer, more resonant. A throb, a pulse. Eyes watching, bodies swaying, hands reaching.

"You know," I said, "my uncle Anton died in this house, in the fire."

"I didn't know," he answered. "I'm sorry. Are you going to be okay to do this?" I shrugged. "I was only five or six when it happened, I barely knew him. Maybe he'll pay us a visit." I stepped back into the hallway, pointed to the oak doors to our left. "What's behind these? A parlour of some kind?"

Stefan turned the handles, pushed them open. Another humid grey cloud exhaled towards us. Every room was like a new living thing, a moist new mouth to walk into.

"This was the games room," he said. "It had a pool table, card tables, a bingo setup. For a while they had Sunday brunches here, and afternoon tea with a fortune teller. Funny old guy. Lived in one of the rooms upstairs."

The funny old guy was my uncle, of course, but I didn't say anything. Stefan walked over to the next stand of worklights, switched them on. They flickered briefly, then blazed to life. This room was the velvet blue of a twilight sky, bubbling away in places, exposing layers of eggshell blue and pale pink beneath. Stefan's eyes turned to the front of the room and he gasped. I steeled myself, let my eyes follow his.

Three large panels of plywood covered the luxuriously large bay window at the front of the room. And on the centre panel, about six feet from the floor, someone had nailed a cat.

It was full-grown, if on the scrawny side. Lifeless, thankfully. And it was hanging from its head on a long steel nail which had pierced the soft underside of the jaw, and then the tongue, and then the palate. The nail had been driven up through the skull so that the crown of the head was against the panel of wood. It would have been difficult to get a living cat into this position, so it was likely dead to start with.

"You had the locks changed after the contractor left?" He nodded. "Then someone has found a way in. Maybe one of the workers who was let go. I doubt they're still here, but we can't be too careful."

"But why would somebody do this?" Stefan asked. He was growing paler by the minute, his breath growing faster and shallower. I took him by the arm, led him out to the hallway, sat him down at the foot of the stairs. "I'm all right, I'm all right," he croaked. He tore the mask from his face, then he reached into his pocket, pulled out an inhaler, huffed once, drew a deep breath—coughed horrendously—then huffed once again. He tossed the mask onto the floor. "These things are useless."

"Don't talk, just breathe," I replied. "It's not as bad out here." However, that was less and less true. The air had thickened in just the last few minutes, stirred up once we started opening doors and moving from room to room. I noted a slight chalky-smoky taste and smell, and for a moment I imagined that we were inhaling remains from the fire, perhaps the ashes of those who had died. Stefan may have pictured this as well—his eyes grew wide with panic, he pulled his plaid cotton handkerchief out of his pocket and held it over his mouth and nose, struggled to slow and deepen his breath. "Maybe you should wait in the car. I won't be long, I promise."

He nodded and pulled himself up with the stair rail. I put my arm around him, helped him to the front door, opened it. The fresh fall breeze pushed back the dust and soot, lightened the air around us. Stefan pulled down his handkerchief and made his way down the front steps, then to the gate. Still wheezing, he turned to me, nodded, then stepped out the gate and headed to a white minivan across the street. I watched a moment longer, then closed the door, and turned around to face the red oak staircase.

"All right," I said aloud. "Enough with the distractions. Let's see what you're really made of."

After a closer look at both the games room and the club/lounge area, I put on the dust mask that Stefan gave me and stepped through the heavy plastic that separated the bar from the kitchen area. The dust was thicker here, hanging in the air. Drywall, sawdust, plaster. Even through the mask I could taste it. The appliances and fixtures were all still in place, in shades of avocado and gold, but a fusty old desk was set up in the centre of the room, stacked with ledgers and registry books, contracts and bills and printed-out emails, old blank membership cards, bank statements and cancelled cheques. A cardboard file box, lid on a nearby chair, was half-filled with yellowing receipts. An ashtray overflowed with cigarette butts, brands that hadn't been sold in years. A door off to the side was helpfully marked BASEMENT. Locked solid.

I put my hand on it, just under the sign, fingertips first then the whole of my palm, and waited. Drew and released a breath. Silent. The whole room was silent, in fact, and rather forlorn. Kitchens were frequent warm spots for residual energies, but not this one.

I looked towards a darkened room off to the side that I assumed would be a pantry, and was startled to see a figure standing there, face half in shadow, staring back at me.

"Hello?" I asked, remembering the cat. I stepped forward—and he did as well—and then I flashed my phone at him and the screen's brightness shone back into my eyes. It was a full-length mirror, attached to the farthest wall. *Jesus Christ, Ivan, you know your own reflection.* I peered into the little room and saw that it had been fashioned into a small dressing area with an arborite makeup table and a metal garment rack replete with plastic, wooden, and wire hangers. I tried to imagine Ethel Merman in here, and couldn't. More likely she took over one of the rooms above and made a loud and boisterous entrance down the stairs.

I stepped back and looked again at the mirror,

touched it. Clouded with dust and icy cold. I did know my own reflection, dammit, and the person in the mirror with the face half in shadow—that person had not been me.

Somewhere above me, something fell to the floor, rolled a little ways, came to a stop. Then silence. *I see I'm being taken on a little tour.* I shrugged, stepped through the sheeting and made my way to the red oak staircase.

"Hello?" I called. "Is someone there?" No one who could answer would, of course, but I found the sound of my own voice reassuring somehow. I started upward and realized that the second floor was also sealed off with plastic and tape, right at the very top stair. Beyond it was a wall of darkness. If there was another stand of worklights up there, I would have to hunt around for it.

My memories of my Uncle Anton were vague and contradictory. I always knew him to be loving and attentive, unlike many of my uncles and aunts—but my most vivid memory was of him shouting at someone (My mother? Their sister?) in Polish or Russian or Ukrainian. Someone was crying, her face hidden—because of the shouting? Or was the shouting because of the crying? Another figure was near, a stranger I think, someone we saw only once. He saw me standing in the doorway, looked across the room at me, and I was instantly afraid.

I remember also that my uncle always carried a deck of cards, and would perform tricks for me—guessing the number, the colour, the suit, and sometimes the face. Or I would take a card from his hand and put it down on the table in front of me, and he would pull the same card from his pocket and reveal that the card on the table had changed. Sometimes he would make me guess the card that he held in his hand, and I would get it right eight, nine, ten times in a row and he would pretend to be amazed.

And I remember his last visit, the last time I saw him, when he came out to the yard where I was playing and sat with me. He said that he was going to be leaving but that he would see me again when he could. He died two nights later. If he knew there would be a fire, why didn't he avoid it or prevent it? Why didn't he save himself?

I felt around for a slit in the sheeting, slipped through it, and headed to the left, pointing the light from my phone screen onto the floor until I found the farthest wall, clad in oak panelling. Above the chair rail was a large blackboard, originally used by the patrons to list their room numbers and sexual come-ons. Now, in a childish hand, the words DIE AIDS FUCKERS were scrawled like a shriek.

I stepped on something, looked down. A small stick of white chalk. This is what I had heard dropping and rolling on the floor earlier. I bent down to pick it up, but then thought better of it and pulled my hand away.

I continued along the far wall, shining my phone from side to side, until I found an electrical outlet, a coil of extension cord, and then the steel tripod of the light stand. I felt around for the switch, snapped it on. Buzzing bright white light everywhere—and greyish white plaster dust everywhere as well.

Nearly all of the original walls on this level had been knocked down but the heavy wooden support posts and beams remained intact. In amongst them, a warren of smaller rooms had been constructed out of drywall and plywood, fitted with plain doors and plain knobs and brassy adhesive room numbers—201, 203, 205 and so on, with the even numbers presumably at the far side of the floor. Some effort had been made to demolish 215, 217 and 219: the doors had been removed and stacked against the far right wall, some of the drywall had been sawn through and disassembled, the frames pulled apart and stacked like cordwood, but the work had stopped abruptly. Room 215 was still half-together—the front wall torn away, the door lying off to one side. A rotted, hollowed-out tooth in a lifeless smile.

I walked through and among the remaining rooms, peering into each one. Some still had bedframes, mirrors, nightstands, but the mattresses all were gone. One room had hooks in the walls for suspending a sling. Here the hum was more like a hiss, a long sigh, hot breath in my ear and on my neck, moist and heavy and close.

A sign on the back wall stated SAUNA AND SHOWERS and pointed off to the left.

I turned the corner and suddenly the darkness rushed to meet me, to wrap me like a blanket and pull me into its embrace. *A man could get lost in here*, I thought, and I turned back towards the light, the stairs, and made my way up to the third floor.

My uncle once told my mother a story that I wasn't supposed to hear, about a drag queen who had performed at the baths. She took a room after her show, stripped out of her clothes and went for a soak in the hot tub, which was located on the third floor deck at the back of the house. She was so tired and the water was so warm, she almost drifted off to sleep, when something round and smooth nudged her leg. She pushed it away with her foot, back into the jets, and then after a moment it bounced back against her again. *Some fool brought a ball in here*, she thought, and then she gave it one more kick. Up popped the body of an old heavy dead man, hairy and wide-eyed, who had apparently had a heart attack a few hours before. "You could hear her screams up the block," he said, laughing, and it was hard not to laugh along with him.

I reached the top of the stairs and turned. The rooms here had been fully dismantled and the remains were placed neatly at the side and back of the cavernous space. Parts of the floor were taped out where the hardwood still needed repair. On the left, a fresh new wall and door led out to the reconstructed deck—with no sign of the hot tub, much to my relief. A single window high in the back let in a single stream of moonlight. Whatever presence was up here was either very weak or very still. For the first time I felt as if I was alone.

Suddenly my phone vibrated in my pocket. I pulled it out to find a text flashing. Stefan's number.

I AM BACK.

Are you feeling better? I replied. No response. I heard a sound behind me. The door to the deck had swung open—I hadn't closed it properly, or it didn't fit well in the frame.

> *Where are you?* I typed. *Stay downstairs, the air is bad up here.*

A pause, and then his answer came through.

> I AM WAITING FOR YOU.

I crossed the room and closed the door, firmly this time, and then locked it. I could just imagine a nest of raccoons moving in and wreaking havoc. The phone vibrated again.

> I HAVE MISSED YOU, it read. IT WAS HIM YOU KNOW. UP FIRE ESCAPE WITH CAN OF GAS.

Who is this? I typed back. *Stefan? Are you okay?*

> SPILLED IT STAIRS AND DOOR. LIT THE MATCH. HE WAS ONLY 12.

> *Stefan, what's going on?*

Then:

STEFAN CANT COME TO THE PHONE.

Who is this? I asked.

A moment, and then:

YOU KNOW.

I stared at the words, afraid to admit their meaning. It was true that Stefan would have been twelve, or close to it, in 1997. And he could have had access to the fire escape and the deck, if someone had lowered the ladder for him. The building's owner for example: his father.

But why? I typed. *Insurance money?*

MAN IN KITCHEN. YOU REMEMBER.

Then:

NICHNI POLITSIYI

The phone went dead.

Outside the wind rose with a low insistent moan. I saw no one, sensed no one, but still I knew to be cautious. The plaster fog seemed thicker now, and oddly sweet in my mouth despite the mask. I stepped around the tape on the floor, made my way to the window, pulled back the stoppers, and pushed up the sash—a gust of cool clear evening air swept in to greet me—and then suddenly a blue-white face on the other side of the screen, milky eyes, gaping mouth, lolling tongue, and then a burst of blackish fluid as it let out a guttural howl—I jumped back, fell back, struck my head on the floor, and plunged into unconsciousness.

I awoke several hours later to discover I'd put my foot through a damaged part of the floor and had broken my ankle. It was too swollen to stand on, never mind walk. My phone was undamaged as far as I could tell, but it had lost its charge completely. I looked behind to where the stairs were, began dragging myself across the floor towards them, and realized as I did so that much of the dust in the air had cleared. I pulled off the mask, tossed it aside, then turned myself so that I could sit on the stairs and move down step by step. This was more painful than I expected, and I had to twist and turn a bit to keep my bad leg from getting jostled or hung up along the way.

As I reached the second floor I noticed that the air had cleared quite a bit there as well. I pushed through the slit in the plastic sheeting and started to bump my way down—only to find Stefan lying face-up on the stairs far below me.

"Stefan?" I called.

He was very still, his face and front were starkly white, as if someone had dumped a bag of flour on him. Step by step I moved down, moved closer, until I was just above him, until I could see that what was covering him was dust, ash and dust, all from the house, and it had filled his mouth and nose and even his ears, until it was spilling out everywhere, until he had choked on it, choked and smothered and died.

I reached over him, picked up his phone, used the tip of his index finger to unlock it. Our last exchange was still on the screen. I deleted our conversation, then switched to the keypad, paused for a moment. Dialled. Clicked over to voicemail.

"Mom?" I said. "I'm okay but I've had an accident, at a worksite downtown. I'm using someone else's phone. Call me back on this number and I'll tell you where to come get me. And maybe don't mention this to Dad."

I hung up—and it abruptly began to ring. Unknown number. Ring and ring. Ring and ring.

"Hello?" I answered.

Silence.

Dial tone.

Then, at the front door, voices rough and urgent, shadows across the pebbled glass. Someone banged their fist repeatedly, rattled the knob, peered inside.

NICHNI POLITSIYI the phone screen flashed. But hadn't I just erased that?

Then all the worklights snapped off.

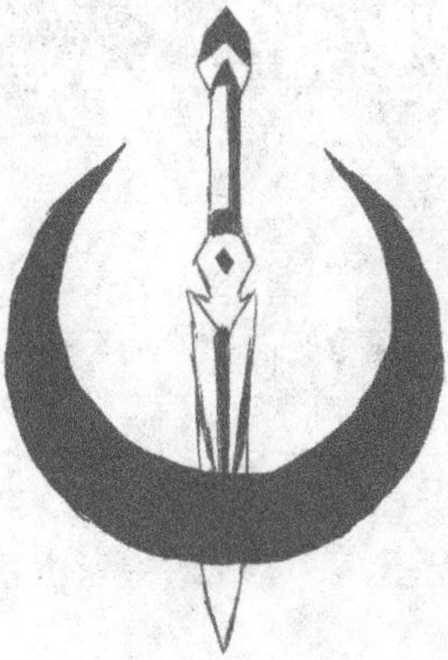

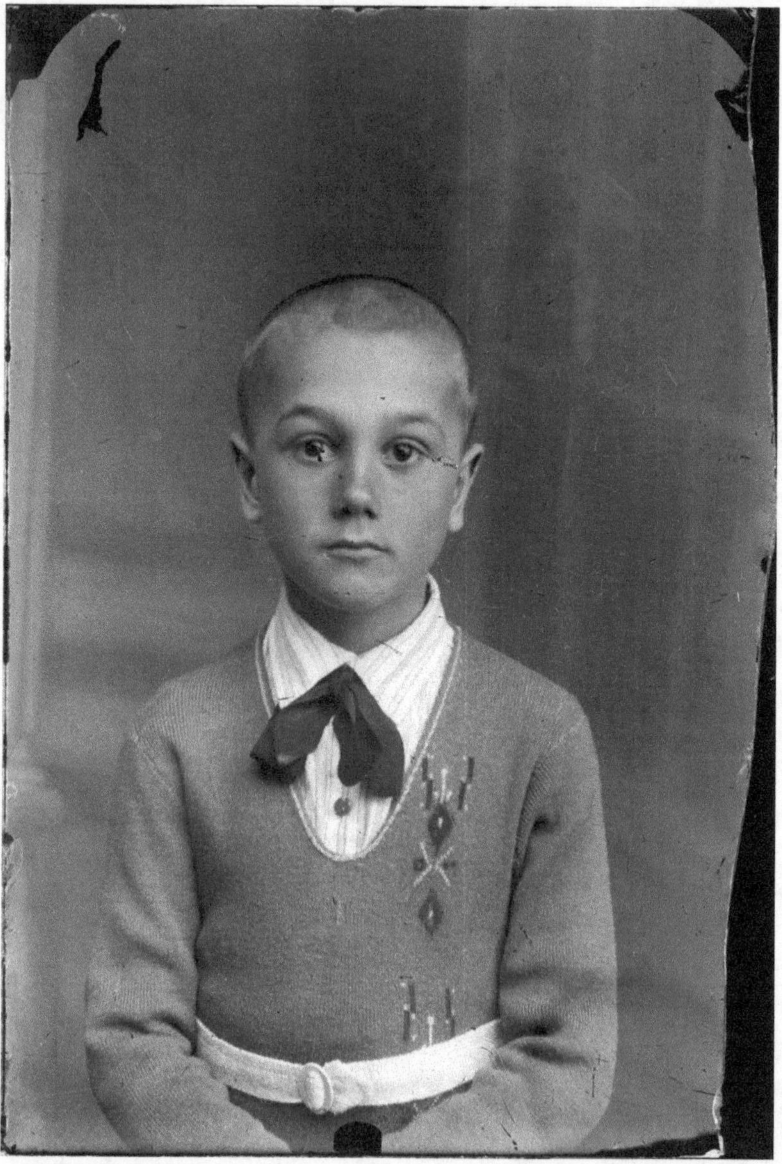

DMITRI

This is all so many years in the past, so you must forgive me. I must have been nine years old when the first of the weekly food trucks came to each of the three villages. This was a few years before the great famine, what much later was known as the *Holodomor*, but even then the crops were beginning to fail and the livestock were struggling. The farms and towns just beyond our region had started to suffer, and the oldest and youngest in every family, in every town, began to sicken and die in greater numbers. It was not unusual for shops to close for days at a time, and for families to have just one meal a day—a few wrinkled potatoes, or a turnip, a half-rotted cabbage, or some beets. At the time, I thought all the villages and towns were visited by trucks providing relief, but I soon learned that, for miles and miles in every direction, our three villages were the only ones being fed.

The trucks were from the Russian army—broad and muscular, loud and angry with metal flaps over the engine that rattled furiously and dusty green tarps fastened tight over the cages that covered the rear beds. Each truck had two armed soldiers in the front and another in the back, all of them gaunt and grave. As the *Holomodor* grew more severe, more soldiers appeared—two, sometimes three in the back and one atop the roof. I remember once when the food truck came hours late—it had been ambushed on the road just outside of our region, more than a dozen people had been killed. And I remember another time when the truck carried the dead body of a soldier in the back, his face covered with a grimy engine rag. He had been caught with one of our apples in his mouth, and he had been shot on the spot. I glimpsed a dark stain on the cloth, shaped like a faraway country, before my mother pulled me away.

"It is the factory," she said as she passed a bowl of borscht to my father. "It has to be." Among the shreds of beets and potatoes and cabbage, chunks of meat nestled like little treasures. Bubbles and swirls of fat glistened on the surface.

"Why does it matter where the food comes from?" my father asked. He plunged his spoon into the bowl, drew out a knot of bone and gristle, set it on a nearby plate.

"I do not want to owe them anything," she replied, setting a steaming bowl down in front of me.

I watched my father move his spoon through the soup in figure-eights, releasing the steam, and I did the same, taking care not to spill.

"What more could we owe than our lives?" he asked, though it wasn't really a question. My father had worked at the factory before I was born. He never spoke of it, and I knew not to ask. He raised a spoonful of soup to his lips and blew gently to cool it. Little red spatters flecked the tablecloth. My mother clucked her tongue, took a slice of bread from the cutting board at the centre of the table, dipped it in the sliced cucumbers and vinegar in a nearby serving dish and dabbed it on the tiny stains.

"Your wife will need to know these things," she said to me, turning her face away from my father. The discussion was apparently over.

A few months later as fall was edging into winter and snow was lightly dusting the fields and roads and trees and houses and outbuildings, I was playing at being a soldier hiding from the enemy in the stand of pines at the border of our property. My parents talked of war when they thought I was asleep—when was it coming, from where, who would fight, who would die. I imagined an enemy squad inching towards our house and I how I would have to pick them off one by one with just my pistol—when suddenly I heard a high, sharp sound, a yelping or mewling, and footsteps thudding, closer and closer. I knelt down behind the tallest and heaviest of the pines and I waited and watched.

This land, on the other side of the pines, was part of the Woytowich farm. Their family was not part of our villages, not even by marriage. They had come to the area from outside Kyiv, had been assigned land by the government, and were told which crops to raise—sugar beets, I believe, which were unsuited to the climate and the soil. They knew they could not seek help from us, so they kept to themselves. I saw their son Adel playing in the fields from time to time, he was close to my age and height, and I saw him now—but he was different, like a stick drawing of a boy, no shoes, shirt open, his skin as white as the fabric that billowed around him. He had a smear of blood on the side of his head, shocking in its brightness. It was he who was making the yelping mewling sounds, running in circles, great clouds of breath bursting out of his mouth, eyes wide, and then I saw that his father was chasing him, holding a large, rough rock. I crouched further down and waited even as my breath fogged the frozen air around me.

Mr. Woytowich was dressed more warmly than his son, in a grey woollen jacket and boots. The boy was weak and shivering and panicked, unsure of how to escape. He turned towards the pines, towards me, but Mr. Woytowich quickly rushed in to block him. The boy backed away, terrified, falling over his own feet.

Just then, a higher, softer voice called his name—"Adel! Adel!"—and his mother appeared over the rise, her head and shoulders cloaked in a faded floral shawl. He started to run to her, then stopped as he saw she was holding a long sharp knife. "Adel, Adel," she beckoned as a loving mother would, but she held the knife out between them, point aimed forward towards the boy, as ready to gut and slice and carve as she was to embrace and console.

He seemed transfixed by her as she moved forward, almost forgetting his father shifting and moving behind him. Suddenly Mr. Woytowich lunged forward, grabbing the boy by the shirt, and just as quickly the boy tore away, rushing first towards his mother and then off to one side as she slashed at the air in front of him. All three were within an arm's length of each other, moving warily. Then wordlessly, Mr. and Mrs. Woytowich began advancing on Adel a step at a time, forcing him to step backward each time they did so. Three steps, four, and then his heel broke through a crust of ice. His ankle turned, his leg crumpled, he fell backward, screaming, and his parents lunged onto him, Mr. Woytowich bringing down the large rough rock, smashing and smashing, and Mrs. Woytowich stabbing with the knife, blood spraying the fine white snow all around them. I watched breathless as they tore at him, pulled his flesh from his bones and gorged on the fresh raw meat, gnashing and chewing and licking and swallowing—then abruptly stopped, hushed themselves, looked from side to side and all around, fearfully, in every direction—then picked up what was left of the boy and hurried back over the rise towards their farmhouse.

I waited and waited until I was sure they were gone, and then I ran home. I sped first past the barn, then around the sheds, I saw my father smoking out back near the clothesline, he saw me and stubbed out his cigarette, I could scarcely speak. "Papa," I rasped, "come quickly, we can't tell Mama."

"She's just putting supper on the table," he said. "I can go with you later." He reached for me and I pulled away.

"No, we have to go now, someone's been killed. You have to come with me."

I didn't need to tell him twice—we ran back up the

way I'd come, my mother calling out behind us but we didn't stop, we ran to the stand of pines where I showed him the welter of blood congealing and freezing into the snow, the trails of footprints weaving around and through each other, and I told him what I saw, I told him everything.

At the end he paused in thought and said, "You are certain it wasn't an animal? You are certain that it was the boy?"

And I answered, "Papa, there are no animals." And it was true: outside our own lands, we hadn't seen boars or rabbits or foxes or deer, or even dogs or cats, not for many days. He nodded, then told me to run home, run without stopping, and stay with my mother inside the house. I was to say there had been an accident, and that we should start supper without him. He would be back as soon as he could. And then he sent me off while he started towards the village.

As my mother and I finished our meal, we could faintly smell something burning. We stepped outside, looked out beyond our fields and saw a thick black ribbon of smoke unfurling from what would have been the Woytowich house. My mother let out a sharp sigh, took my hand and led me back inside. An hour later, my father returned and sent me to bed, then told my mother the whole story as I lay wide awake listening. He had brought a half-dozen men to the Woytowich house. They had found the husband and wife, they had found what was left of their son. They beat the couple until they were close to death and then set them afire, and then stood outside and watched as their house burned to the ground.

That night I had a terrible dream, which I knew in my heart to be true, and in that dream I was back among the pines, huddled close to the ground, watching Adel as he was chased by his father and then by his mother—and in the moment before he fell backward, his eyes turned to the pines and he saw me, and I saw him, and his eyes locked with mine and said, "Help me." I could have done something, I could have shouted, I could have thrown a handful of stones, I could have rushed in and grabbed at the knife. I could have been a soldier. I woke up bathed in sweat, my parents hovering over me. I said I remembered nothing.

My mother's sister Mimi came to visit a few days later, unannounced, she had been born in the village but now lived in Kyiv. She never watched what she said around me, she said the city stank of death and that she had sold everything and spent everything to make her way back to us. So of course we took her in. She held me tight against her and told my mother that in Kyiv there were handbills pasted to the sides of buildings: « Їсти власних дітей – це варварство » they read. "Eating your children – it is barbarism."

I asked Aunt Mimi what barbarism was, but my mother answered instead. "It is worse than what animals do, that is what it is." And she gave us both sharp looks. Still, we ate our stew that night, food from the trucks, and I thought as we ate that it was exactly like what animals did, it was only worse because it was us.

And I can tell you one more thing. The boy Adel was three months younger than me, nine years and four months when he was killed—and the time in our villages when so few were born, the time we call *Movchanya*, it lasted just over nine years. It might be a coincidence. Or I might be misremembering. All this, as I said, was many years ago. And cannibalism is everywhere now, everywhere you look, you can scarcely walk a block. Decent people, out in the open. I fear for what will come next.

DACIAN

Years later, as I was driving through the streets of Warsaw, slick with freezing rain, I heard one of the old songs on the radio, one that we had danced to in the church hall the night we met. *Two roses, faded, in a crystal vase.* I pulled my car over to the side of the road and listened, and as I did so I felt the lightest brush of her fingertips on the back of my neck. I gasped and jumped away, my flesh crawling at the thought. I spun around, my eyes searching the back seat, searching everywhere. I was alone. I turned back to see the rain had turned to heavy wet snow. I switched off the radio, put the car into gear, then turned the rearview mirror away from me, afraid of what I might see. Slowly, fearfully, I drove back towards my home, which had been our home. I thought I smelled lilacs but that was impossible—the first blooms were still weeks away.

She had been born in a small farming town where Ukraine borders Romania. Both her parents were dead. This was as much as I knew of her past, or at least it is what she had claimed. Her childhood, her family, her friends, her journey that brought her to Poland, every question I asked was met with icy silence. But in every other way she was open and joyful, bright eyes and full mouth, flaxen hair and satin skin. Everywhere we went, the colours seemed to shimmer and dance like music for the eyes, the sounds of the city sparkled in our ears, and we were bundled together in a love that wrapped us and warmed us against a world growing colder. It was as if the whole city was under her spell, and we were all seeing the world and each other with new eyes.

I do not know why I killed her. One moment she was alive in my arms, laughing, my hand on the back of her neck, laughing, my other on her throat, laughing louder, and then I was squeezing, tighter and tighter, and her laughter rang out all around us even after she was dead on the floor. Her eyes wide and empty. Her darling mouth twisted into a rictus. Had she been laughing, or crying? Or screaming? Where had we been—at dinner, a nightclub, out on the street? It was as if everything before this moment had been a dream, and now, for the first time in years, with her crumpled body before me, now I was fully awake.

"Do it," I remember her saying as she laughed in my face. "You'll never be rid of me. Do it and I'll be yours forever." I could see her daring me, mocking me—but I could also see her pleading with me. *Do it*, she gasped, tears streaming down her cheeks. Which was real? Which was the dream? It mattered little. I was a murderer now, a monster, and I had to conceal my crime. I waited till well after midnight, then bundled her in blankets and carried her to the car, laying her gently across the back seat. I drove north along the river until it was nearly light, and then I placed her at the water's edge, face down, so that she was just barely submerged. It felt like a thousand eyes were trained on me, that at any moment someone would come and stop me, but no one saw me and no one came. And no one ever found her.

This was the odd thing. No one ever found her. Every day and night I waited for the knock at the door, the hand on my shoulder. *Come with us please, we have some very sad news.* But no such news came. A week later, I broke down, did the foolish thing, the stupid thing, I drove back up the river to where I had left her, and of course she was gone, not a trace. So someone had found her, or she had washed away. She couldn't just get up and leave.

That first night when we met and danced, she pulled herself close and whispered "You will soon love me," and her words came true—as the hours passed and sunrise grew near, I knew I would never leave her. The first time we made love, my hands slid down her back, my fingers moved along her spine and found a series of indentations, on either side, like tiny mouths. My finger slipped into one, and something uncoiled inside. "Careful," she murmured and kissed my forehead, and the memory slipped away. A week later,

I think, I came home from work early to find her in the kitchen on the floor eating a child, just four or five years old, gutting it, devouring it, the still-breathing body twitching and shuddering. Did this happen? I don't know. What do I remember? So many fragments jagged and broken—as if a beautifully painted glass had smashed and, when the pieces have fallen away, a vile and monstrous image was revealed.

As I drove in the rain, the mirror facing away from me, one image after another sprang from the depths of my mind to confront me. What day was it when she tore at herself, screaming "Why am I alive?" and pushed me away when I tried to hold her? What night was it when I woke to find her curled up in the corner staring blankly, blood caked down the front of her face? When was it that we came home from a night out to find the windows smashed and the floors all covered with dead birds, bloodied, their necks all broken? Were these even my memories? Or was the dream of our life together now turning, curdling in my guilt-wracked brain?

Suddenly I felt smooth soft hands slide over mine to grab the wheel, felt a lithe and dainty foot press onto mine to push the accelerator, watched helplessly as we approached the chiming train crossing, saw the crossing gate start its downward swing, rushed towards the tracks to meet the charging engine, her warmth so close, her voice so close, *Do it*, almost a kiss, a precious kiss, the whistle screech, the blinding lights, *Do it do it and you'll be mine, you'll be mine forever.*

MIHAELA

Knitting is a good way to pass the time when you're waiting for something to die.

I learned to knit from Mrs. Yelchin, who would sit with me while my mother went shopping or visiting, often on Saturday afternoons. Over the many weeks of visits, I learned to make stockings, hats, mittens and gloves, lace shawls and scarves. Mrs. Yelchin was already very old and, while she never said so, I can now look back and see that she wanted company as her final days crept closer. One morning when I was twelve, a few months before we left the village for Bucharest, my mother heard that Mrs. Yelchin had taken ill suddenly and had died in the night. At my mother's urging, I finished the Russian lace shawl that I had been working on and sent it to her daughter with my condolences. I later learned that the daughter had been ill as well, and died just a few weeks after. I was told she was buried wearing the shawl, but I cannot be certain.

Once we arrived in Bucharest, a strange fear came over me that grew stronger and sharper every day: I became convinced that I had stopped growing. Other girls my age were now taller, rounder, becoming young women. I was not. I ate, I slept, my heart pumped, my lungs drew air, but I was somehow frozen in time. Even my hair, my fingernails. Of course I didn't tell anyone—my parents, my friends, my teacher. What could I say? But as the season changed from summer to autumn and my mother brought out my warmer clothes, she looked and saw that I could still fit into everything, that none of my dresses or blouses or skirts needed to be let down or let out.

"Who has been cutting your hair, Mihaela—have you been using my good scissors?" No, I replied, no one's cut my hair. "Well, that's impossible," she said, looking at it left and right—then oddly, defiantly, picked up the scissors, pinched a length of my hair between her fingers and snipped it. Still holding my hair, she set the scissors down, looked back and gasped. The hair was restored, as if it had never been touched. Yet there were the cuttings, in her lap, blonde and gleaming. Startled, she brushed them off of her dress and onto the floor as if they were the legs of spiders.

By winter it was obvious that something was wrong, and my mother pulled me from school. From then until I was twenty, I rarely left the house and only when accompanied. My father was unconcerned at first, but came to realize the implications and made arrangements for me to see a doctor. My mother quickly persuaded him to cancel, fearing that I would be subjected to tests and experiments, diagnosed as a freak or in some way abnormal, and then seized and shut away in a hospital or sanitarium. Articles in the newspapers spoke of the quest for genetic purity, the forced sterilization of the mentally and physically unfit. And so I went unexamined, and my mother taught me at home.

And then my father was killed—run down by a drunken soldier in a military vehicle. There was no restitution, barely even an admission that the accident had occurred. My mother and I would soon be penniless. He had been a violinist in a chamber orchestra, supported by a selection of wealthy older patrons. My mother knew some of them, and they in turn knew others. And so I was introduced to a series of men with specialized tastes who would pay my mother for the pleasure of my uniquely diminutive company.

For even as my twenty-first birthday approached, I remained ageless, never physically developing and in some ways never emotionally maturing. Over the next two decades, I spent nights or weekends with dozens of men, some of whom wanted to use me cruelly, to live out unspeakable fantasies, and others who just wanted to talk or play. At first it was troubling, but I came to feel that I was in some way helping to prevent the mistreatment of actual children by simulating one for these men. I later feared that I was doing the opposite—fuelling appetites rather than sating them, creating victims instead of sparing them.

In the end, it came down to this: we needed the money. My mother was elderly, and dying, and in a private hospital. The war was raging around us. The chief physician, Leo, who had been one of my earliest patrons, now played at being my uncle and lover and thankfully was all but impotent. I would spend mornings in my mother's one-room flat, preparing and packing a lunch, then afternoons at her bedside, feeding her and then knitting a feathery shawl for her shoulders and arms as she often complained of draughts. In the evenings I would dine with Leo and spend a few hours in his home, watching him drink and smoke and mutter about his deceitful colleagues until he collapsed into a heap on one piece of furniture or another. I would then let myself out and ask his driver to return me to my residence. Then, one afternoon, as I approached the shawl's last rows, my mother died beside me with barely a sound. I looked up at her slack face, her clouding eyes, and I knew. I promptly stood up, touched her cheek lightly, then went down to the driver and requested a ride back to Leo's apartments.

Once there, I asked the driver to come up for a moment and help me with my bags. He was surprised to see them already packed and waiting. I gave him one hundred rubles from my mother's purse and told him to drive me to a small church on the eastern edge of the city—and to say nothing to Leo of my whereabouts. At the church was another old patron of mine who, after a substantial donation, was kind enough to send me to a convent in Valea Vinului, where I have been ever since.

I am quite old now, perhaps too old. I have outlived all the sisters I met when I first came here. It is my own death that I wait for, if death can ever come for me, and I knit to pass the time. We have a cook that we've taken in, a young woman from a nearby town who bore a daughter out of wedlock. The girl is ten years old. I spend the mornings helping her with her studies, then in the afternoons we play together in the courtyard, and in the evenings I teach her how to knit. With her, I am a child again, with still so much to learn.

GFA

NADIYA

I was only out of the room for a moment, but when I came back she was gone.

My husband Emil and I had separated five months earlier when I became aware that he was seeking out the companionship of young men. A pederast, this was the word at the time. Such behaviour was not unknown to me—I would join my friends for evenings at the theatre and the Kyiv Opera and we would often gossip about which actors and singers were more interested in each other than in their leading ladies. Still, it was a criminal act, and his activities were dangerous to us both. While I loved my husband, I could not compromise my desire for a complete marriage, nor could I risk being seen as his accomplice. And so we parted, amicably and discreetly. He set me up in a flat on Reitarska Street in the old city, and deposited a monthly stipend into a separate account in my name. But my daughter and I never saw him again.

Larysa was quite young, only seven years old, and she missed her father terribly, asking for him over and over. She took to spending more time alone, playing with her dolls and looking at picture books and talking to herself, telling little stories.

I once caught her standing in front of my bedroom mirror laughing and smiling and asking it if she was pretty. "Do you think I am pretty?" were the words that she said. When I stepped into the room, she blushed and turned away as if she'd been caught doing something shameful. There was something about this moment that I almost recognized, it was like a word on the tip of my tongue, but I brushed it off and told her not to play with my things, to go to her own room and prepare for bed.

A few days after, my mother sent a telegram asking us to come to Odessa for a beach holiday—our tickets would be waiting for us at Central Station on the 23, just one week away. I stopped in at the school a few minutes early so that I could advise them of our travel plans.

The administrator smiled and took me aside, then said, "Your daughter is finally coming out of her shell, I see. She was so quiet at the start of the year but now she chatters constantly—your new nanny seems to have made a difference."

I was just about to tell her that she was mistaken, that we had no nanny, when suddenly Larysa appeared at the office door, smiling and excited, with a fresh drawing in her hand. I decided to let the matter lapse, and thanked the administrator for her time. As we were leaving the building I asked Larysa if I could see the drawing. She unfolded it and handed it to me. It was a woman, tall and handsome with a waist like a wasp, a long black skirt, black jacket, black gloves and a smart black hat. She was surrounded by small shadows. At first I thought they were tombstones but then realized they were the silhouettes of many small children. “Who is this?” I asked. “Is this your new nanny?”

“Yes,” she answered. “She lives in the mirror with all of the other children and she visits me every night.” Once again I felt that there was something familiar about this, something smouldering in the back of my mind, something just out of reach. However, I knew that children her age often created imaginary friends and playmates for themselves, especially after a loss. I forced a smile and looked at the picture once more.

“Well, she seems very pleasant,” I ventured. “Does your nanny have a name?”

“Her name is Miss Skovanka, and she wants to watch over me always.” She held out her hand to me and I instinctively reached for it, then realized what she wanted was the drawing. I folded it and passed it back to her, and she clutched it to her chest as the wind began to whip around us. I placed my hand on her back but she shrugged it away.

“Miss Skovanka is very kind to take such an interest in you. I think we can take care of you together. I can be with you during the day, and she can watch you at night. How would that be?”

Larysa furrowed her brow and kept looking forward as we walked. “She said always,” was her reply, which struck me as impertinent, but then I remembered how difficult these months had been and how few friends she had, at school or on the street. A nanny could be just what Larysa needed, even if she did not exist.

That evening, between supper and bedtime, Larysa was in her room reading to herself, singing little songs, chittering about her day at school. I was pleased that she was no longer sullen and silent, but I felt a vague unease that she was sharing these childish moments with a figment. I was half out of my chair to ask her to come sit with me when suddenly she let out a shriek. I vaulted across the room, threw open her door and saw that the shoulder on her night dress was torn. "What's happened?" I asked. "Have you hurt yourself?"

"We were playing a game, Miss Skovanka and I, and she reached out and tried to catch me." She had her hand over her shoulder, and beneath I could see her skin was red and raw and scratched. *She has done that to herself*, I thought as I pulled her close against me. *She wants to use Miss Skovanka to gain my attention. Perhaps the nanny has outgrown her usefulness, and Larysa needs my help to let her go*. I looked around the room. Unlike the full-length glass across from my bed, Larysa had only the modest square mirror above her dresser. For a moment I thought I caught, out of the corner of my eye, a face, a shadow, but no, it was nothing. A trick of the light in a darkening room.

"I am sure that Miss Skovanka meant you no harm," I said. "But, if you like, you can come sleep in my bed tonight."

"Yes please," she said, holding me tighter. And I smiled. After so many years of doubt and worry, it seemed I knew something about raising a child after all.

I tidied the flat and turned out the lights, Larysa following along like a kitten, then pulled on a nightdress and slipped into bed, and she nestled against my back, away from the mirror, her warmth for a moment reminding me of Emil and what I missed most from him. I listened as her breathing slowed, sigh upon sigh upon sigh. I kept my eyes trained on my bedroom mirror, on my dim reflection across from me, until I too fell asleep.

I awoke with a start. No more than two or three hours had passed. The room was so black I wondered if I had gone blind—but then faint outlines of the furnishings emerged from the darkness. I realized that Larysa was no longer curled against me. I felt around behind me. I was alone under the coverlet. "Larysa?" I whispered.

I heard her before I saw her. As my sight adjusted, I perceived that she was seated on the floor across from the mirror, naked and shivering, rocking herself, gasping and muttering, strange sounds, strange words. A troubling private ritual. Did she know where she was? Was she even awake? "Larysa?" I whispered again.

I pulled the cover from the bed, knelt down beside her and wrapped them around the two of us. "Mummy?" she said, as if waking from a distant dream. "Mummy, Miss Skovanka said she was sorry, she would never hurt me, it was just a game."

"Of course it was, dear." She was still half in a trance—fever, chills, beads of sweat. Had she been ill all this time and I just hadn't realized? The room was suddenly so warm, so close, I thought I might faint myself. I stood up and made my way to the tall hinged windows that faced out onto the street, unlatched and opened them as far as their flat steel chains would allow. I hurried out the door to fetch a glass of water for Larysa—and once again, as I passed the mirror, I saw, I felt I saw, *something*, a flicker, a presence—I shook my head to clear it, rushed to the kitchen, the sink, the cupboard, found and filled a cut glass goblet, the survivor of a set Emil had found for us years ago. I rushed back, tripping over my own feet, pushed open the door and Larysa was gone. The quilt lay in a rumpled crescent on the floor. The bed was empty, as was its underside. The windows would not, could not, open far enough for her to fall or jump out. The wardrobe was empty.

"Larysa?" I called. Was she in the washroom? No. Was she back in her own room? No. The hallway, the closets, the living room, dining room, pantry—"Larysa?"—then I stopped. I heard a faint chuckle, like the rustle of dry leaves. *Hide and Seek!* I thought to myself. *All just a game!* "Larysa, where are you?" I ran back to the bedroom—that chuckle again—then a scattering of giggles, high and sharp and biting. I glanced in the mirror, without even meaning to, and I glimpsed, just a flash: All of them, the little shadows, and centred among them, with one hand on Larysa's shoulder and the other over her mouth, was Miss Skovanka, tall and thin and pale with hard cold eyes and a crimson slash for a mouth. She smiled at me, an impossible smile, and stepped back into the darkness, pulling Larysa in with her.

The police came and went. They were led by an odd little man in a uniform I did not recognize. His Russian was forced and foreign. Abduction was what he surmised. I could not persuade him otherwise—and, with no forced entry apparent, my estranged husband was the sole suspect. I telegraphed my mother and advised her I would be travelling alone, and would explain why once I arrived. But when I stepped up to the ticket counter and showed my identification, the clerk handed me my ticket and also an envelope—a reply from her which merely said "I know." The next morning, when I arrived at Odessa Station, my mother was waiting on the platform with her driver, and this was the story she had to tell as we drove to her home near Lanzheron:

"I am not surprised you have forgotten, as you were very small, but when you were a girl a friend of yours vanished in just the same way as Larysa. Several children disappeared—we thought at first it was a murderer, but then we heard the stories from our own families. This goes back many years for us, decades, even centuries.

"As you know, our land has suffered many invasions and annexations. It was not uncommon for husbands to be killed, wives and children to be taken and enslaved. There are tales of women who resisted and fled, who hid in the dense Carpathian woods and made their own lives there as thieves, prostitutes, anchorites, healers, and seers. One was known for gathering orphans, concealing them and protecting them from predacious, murderous soldiers. She was known as *Dama Shkovanka*, or 'Miss Hiding Place.'

"Of course, as these stories too often unfold, she was observed and followed by a clutch of hussars back to her home, and when she refused to release the children into their custody, the soldiers slaughtered them in front of her, and then tortured and killed her as well. Forever after, it is said, she will torment their descendants, taking some of their children for her own. How she chooses, when and why, we do not know. But her eyes are always on us, from within mirrors, from behind picture-glass, and in the reflections on polished silver and tin. She watches and she waits. She calls to our young ones in a voice that only they can hear, she gains their trust and pulls them in—for her loneliness is insatiable, and she craves their company. I would have dismissed this as a fantasy if I had not seen the effects myself. And, too late, I tell you now what I thought you already knew."

We passed much of our visit in grief and in silence. I sat cloistered inside the house, in corners, away from the light. I found my eyes searching over every shining surface in hopes of spying my daughter's face looking back at me. And then, when I returned to my flat, I could not stop myself: I threw open the door to Larysa's bedroom and into it I moved every mirror of every size, every hanging glass, every metal tray and cup and vase—hundreds and thousands of rubles I spent in corner shops and antique stores until all four walls were covered, every surface—and each night I sat on her bed and prayed that she would show herself. I do it still, I will do it tonight. I sit and watch and wait, as Miss Skovanka once watched me.

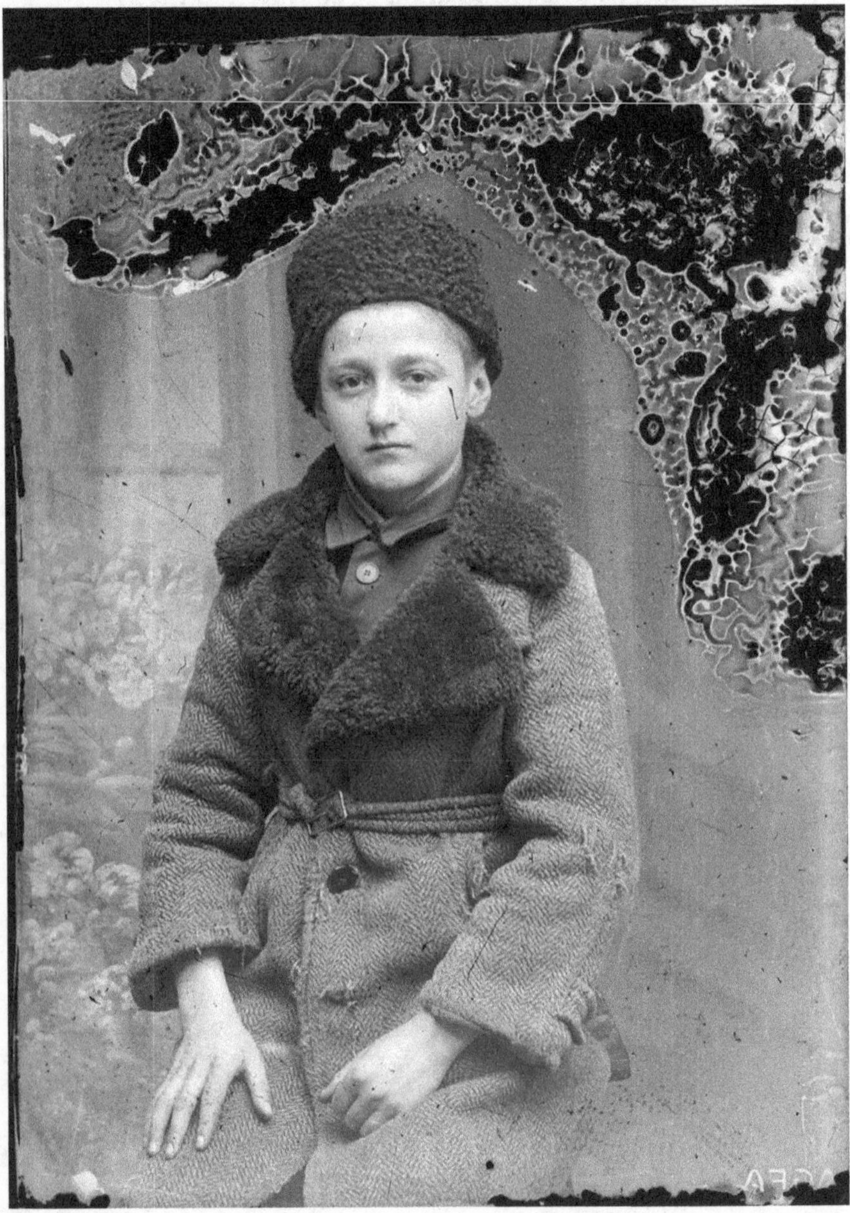

DRAGOI

When I was thirteen, shortly after the end of the war, my mother and sister and I moved from the eastern village all the way to Krakow, where my Aunt Polina lived. Both my father and Polina's husband had been killed in recent battles, and Polina had found a house where we, the widows and children, could live together. While she and my mother had never been close, they were lonely and afraid now and faced an uncertain future. Polina, in particular, feared retaliation for her German husband's Nazi ties, had apparently removed her rings, destroyed her wedding certificate and had returned to her maiden name. My mother hoped that a new home would be a new start, and that we could support each other in whatever challenges we faced.

And yet: even though her driver met us at the train station and brought us to her home, Polina rushed to the door in a panic as if she'd forgotten we were coming. She pushed the key to the new house into my mother's hand, stammered something about unexpected guests, and then had the driver take us away without her. We drove off in uneasy silence, weaving through the streets until we pulled up in front of an unassuming house on Ulica Szeroka. As the driver brought our cases up the steps, he assured us that Polina was preparing to join us, and would do so at her earliest opportunity.

She never did. Later that night, perhaps when the driver turned the key in the lock, or when my sisters and I pulled the dust cloths from the worn but elegant antique furniture, or when my mother tucked us into our freshly changed beds, Aunt Polina fell down her cellar stairs shrieking and tearing at herself, had a heart attack, and died.

A few days after the funeral, my mother was upstairs bathing my sister and I was sitting alone in the kitchen, when I heard a strange sound coming from the basement. As if an animal had somehow gotten trapped and was whining to be freed. In our previous house, a fox came into the cellar through a loose window and smashed some jars of my mother's beets and sauerkraut. I called out for her but she couldn't hear me. I decided to be brave and go downstairs to see if it was a fox, and perhaps I could release it. I knew it might be rabid, so I put my gloves on just in case.

The staircase down was narrow, with pantry shelves along one side, stocked with canned goods. Nothing behind them. The animal sound was coming from farther down, somewhere behind the stairs. I reached the floor, put my hand out towards the centre of the room, feeling for the beaded chain of the ceiling light. I found it, pulled it, splashed the room with harsh white light. In the corner behind the stairs was a new-looking coal furnace. Could something have come down the chimney? As I moved closer, my gloved hands ready for the capture, I realized the sound was of someone sobbing. Someone beside or behind the furnace. Someone I couldn't see. I drew closer still, looked one way and then another. No one was there, I was alone, but still I could hear it—coming, it seemed, from within the wall.

The rest of the basement was lined with stone, but this corner was built over with brick. I leaned in towards those on the staircase wall, as this was where the sound was the loudest—and suddenly one brick fell out, was pushed out, and then another, and I could see in, and what I saw was a hand. A large, thick-fingered hand, gloved perhaps like mine. And then the fingers moved.

I flew up the stairs and crashed into my mother, almost knocking her down. I could barely form words, I was so frightened. My mother told my sister, still wet and wrapped in her towel, to go back upstairs and wait while we investigated. Normally she would have protested but she could see the fear in my face, and went back up to our bedroom.

I shushed my mother as we crept down the stairs, brought her around and pointed at the bricks, at the hole in the wall. She moved slowly with me, and then closer to the hole, peered into it. "See?" I asked. "See the fingers?" She nodded—then reached in, touched the hand.

"Clay," she said. "It's made of clay."

"I saw it move!" I said. "I heard it crying!"

She gave me a stern look and was about to scold

me—when the sobbing began once more. She looked at the wall, and then looked at me. "I know what this is," she said. "And I know who we must call." She ushered me back towards the stairs. I reached for the chain but she stopped me. "Leave the light on," she said. "And be careful on the steps."

Two days later, very early in the morning, my mother answered a knock at the door and welcomed in an old woman, older than any I had ever known or seen. I never knew where she came from, or what her name was. The way she moved and spoke made me think of our village home but I did not remember ever meeting her. My mother handed her a small cloth bag which she tucked into her coat pocket, and then she walked directly to the kitchen and down into the basement. None of us followed.

My legs ached from standing by the time she returned, though she could only have been gone a few minutes. She did not even try to take my mother aside—she addressed her directly in front of us, and this is what she said.

"You must leave, before nightfall if at all possible. You can come back to the borderlands with me, if you wish. This is a stolen house, as is every chair and table and bed and bucket within its walls, stolen and now cursed. It belongs to the Yevrei, and the creature downstairs is a Golem—formed of clay by a master of the Kabbalah to protect the wife and child who lived here before you. The husband was taken by soldiers and executed; it is his soul which inhabits the monstrosity, and it is his heart that breaks with grief. For his wife and child were taken before he could possess the statue, and now they too are dead. He is trapped here, filled with rage and despair. You are in peril if you stay."

"You say this house is stolen," said my mother, "but my sister Polina bought this house, she bought it for us to live in together."

"Your sister bought it from a thief, and she knew she was doing so. She knew the house, she came to see it while the family still lived here. She was the first victim of the Golem, and the thief who arranged the sale was the next. The Golem bears you no ill will, but he cannot let you stay."

"But you must be able to undo this," my mother said. "Release his spirit, send him away."

"I cannot," the old woman answered. "This is not our work, and it is not ours to undo. You would need to find the Kabbalist who conjured him. That of course is impossible now. Millions of the Yevrei are dead, and those that are not have escaped to other lands. He is condemned to live here forever, alone."

After a long silence, her eyes cast downward, my mother spoke. "I will pack our things," she said. "We will leave with you."

"I must tell you," the old woman sighed, "that the creature wants to see your boy. He will not be harmed. It should only take a moment." She looked at me, reached out to take my hand.

"Have you gone mad?" my mother exclaimed. "Leave that monster alone with my child?"

"It is a monster with the soul of a man. Or, if you

prefer, a man with the capabilities of a monster. Either way: It is a request that you cannot deny."

I took the old woman's hand and went with her down the stairs, slowly and carefully, to face the creature in the wall.

The bricks had now all fallen away, and I could see him fully from head to toe. He was terrifying in his stature, yet imbued with a strange beauty and created with obvious care. The old woman led me to stand at his feet, and he trembled all over. I was afraid he might shake himself apart. His tears had dug deep grooves from the corners of his eyes down his cheeks to his jaw.

"You were a good man," I told him, as if speaking to my own father. "You must forgive yourself."

The old woman reached across to him, pulled a piece of clay from the tip of the smallest finger on his left hand. She formed it into a ball, and handed it to me.

"This clay will always be alive," she said. "It will never dry or crack. And its spirit will always be with you. Take this, and always remember."

It has been many years. My mother is long dead. I have married, as has my sister. She has two daughters, and I have a son. We live in different cities now, all of us. I still have the ball of clay. It has neither dried nor cracked, and when I hold it, I still feel the life inside.

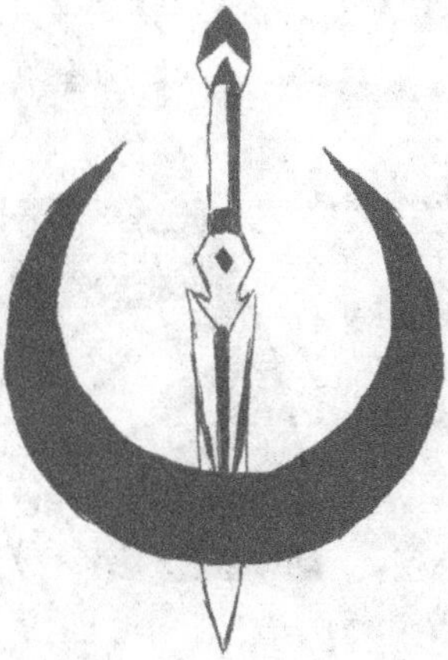

ОНА

LENA

Alice once asked: "If you were a monster, what kind would you be?" This was on our first real date, not just a coffee or a walk through a park. We had gone out for a big sushi dinner served in one of those wooden "love boats" and then had walked back through the narrow streets, shimmering and slippery with fresh icy rain. It was supposed to be funny but something about the question, the tone, made me uneasy. I wasn't sure how I should answer. She put her arm around me, pulled me closer. "You know," she added. "A vampire, a werewolf, a mummy." I knew. Believe me, I knew.

"A sea monster, I think," I replied. "I love the water, I love to swim. I'd be happy in a black lagoon."

Many times my aunt Maryan told me a story from the old country about a young girl whose sailor brother was taken by a sea witch and hidden in a twisting winding tangle of caves under an island of barren rock. Unlike the slender pale lake spirits in her other tales from the first land, the sea witch was a voluptuous woman with the lush full tentacles of a giant squid, and she would search the ocean for shipwrecked sailors to take back to her lair, where she would mate with them—somehow—and then eat them alive. The witch was beautiful and regal and solitary and voracious. I had always wanted to be her. I considered telling Alice this, but from what little I knew of dating, it didn't seem like ideal conversation.

I turned and looked at her, pulled a long lock of hair away from her forehead. "What about you, what kind would you be?"

"What makes you think I'm not one already?" Then she widened her mouth, baring her teeth, as she made a dark gurgling sound, and lunged for my neck, laughing and laughing until we both nearly fell into the street.

I knew very little about dating before I met Alice, only what I'd read in books or seen at the movies. It was odd, one minute I was alone in my library carrel, the next she was hovering over me, introducing herself and asking what I was reading (*Jane Eyre*), what I was wearing (a simple summer dress that had been my mother's), and if I would like to join her in the cafe downstairs for some tea. Tea on Tuesday led to more tea and a walk in the park on Friday, and then the sushi dinner that Sunday.

One thing I didn't know about dating was that you had to answer so many questions about yourself, some of them very personal. Was I in school? (No, I was schooled at home by my aunt.) Where did I work? (I didn't, and probably wouldn't, I had what I guessed was called a fixed income.) Where did my money come from? (An inheritance from my aunt's family, we received a payment every month.) What did I do with my days? (I went to the library, or to the cinema, or I walked or swam.) Alice answered my questions easily, and I realized she had probably dated a few people before me, so she was already prepared. For me, it was like the game shows on TV, where if you said the right words in the right order at the right time, you would win a prize.

It was on our way back to Alice's home from the park, we were walking along the edge of the market talking about favourite toys we'd had as children (I had a stuffed clown with a rubber face that played a lullaby when you wound its red plastic nose) when something sprayed onto a wall caught my eye: a blast of pinkish purple, a stencil or some kind of graffiti with some garbled lettering above it. A wiry guy with a ponytail was standing next to it, postering for a band night at a bar up the street.

"What's that?" I said to her as we reached the corner—then I felt something, a twitch and a tickle, low on my back, as if someone had just put their hand there. Little Sprout was awake. That was a bad sign. Had it smelled something, brushed against something? I glanced behind, looked around—nothing—then Alice piped up from my right, "What's what?"

"That over there," I said, gesturing towards the wall across the street, but whatever I'd seen was gone. Long-haired guy was slapping wheat paste over where the spray had been, or where I thought it had been, and then smoothed another swath of posters down on top of it.

"I guess it's under there now, it was . . . odd." I hadn't seen it clearly, I couldn't have described it. An ad of some kind? Or some kind of art? Or maybe a warning, like those interlocked circles on drums of hazardous waste. I looked from wall to wall to doorway to fence to see if I could find another, but there was nothing similar in sight. The twitch at the small of my back had subsided, replaced with a low dull throb. *Little Sprout*, I whispered in my head, *go back to sleep*.

"Are you okay?" she asked. "You seem a bit shaky."

"I should head home," I said. "My aunt will be wondering where I am." The image had been right over there—but what had it been? I barely saw it, it shouldn't have mattered, but somehow it did and I didn't know why. As if I alone was meant to see it and, for a moment, I had. I walked Alice to the door of her building, gave her a light goodnight kiss on the lips—a first for me—and watched as she unlocked the front door and made her way up the stairs.

By the time I got home, Maryan was already in bed. She was quite old now, and almost always asleep by nine. My back was sore but not painful, and the twitching had stopped completely. I would have to be careful sleeping, though, and then be sure to have her take a look in the morning. I felt like something had happened, not just there but inside me as well, something had tugged loose and was trying to free itself. Little Sprout. Maryan would know what to do. I gently closed her bedroom door, then walked quietly through the kitchen and down the stairs, past the laundry room and into my apartment.

Maryan was my late mother's half-sister, and it was in her house that I lived. I had a small flat in the basement with my own kitchen and bathroom as well as a separate entrance, up a small flight of cement steps and out into the back yard, which allowed me to come and go without too much disruption. It had been difficult moving even this far from her, though we both knew it was a necessity. She had raised me almost from birth, alone, and was unable to see me as anything other than the little girl she taught to read and write and sing.

My restlessness throughout my teenage years had troubled her greatly: my disappearance for hours at a time; my constant travels through the city, by bus and train and bike and on foot; my late-night swims from the docks to the scattering of islands in the centre of the lake; my pre-dawn stumblings through the house and my long early morning showers scrubbing and scrubbing at myself with undisguised self-hatred. Like many mothers and daughters, she and I would fight our way around the real problems between us. She had raised me to become the person I was meant to be, and now that person confused and angered her, and sometimes frightened her.

A girl went missing last year—fourteen and drunk, she had fallen from one of the party boats in the heat of the summer and her body just vanished. She had been alone on the deck, she had gone up looking for something or someone. It was all the city could talk about, divers searched for her for days while Maryan scowled at me, unable to say anything, unable to ask.

Finally, a week later, the girl's body washed up three miles away, once pretty, now blue and bloated, shrouded in weeds and wreathed with snails. *Full fathom five, thy father lies; of his bones are coral made; those are pearls that were his eyes.* Her eyes were gone—alas, no pearls—and part of her face scraped down to the bone, to the teeth. And, most vividly, her left leg, gone. Gnawed and slashed and torn away, perhaps by a propeller blade, or caught between rocks, still somewhere amid the filth and debris lining the harbour bed.

Suddenly, just as I had pulled my pyjama top over my head and was reaching to switch off the light, I heard a shuffle, a stumble, from the floor above me. "Maryan?" I called. Something fell to the floor with a thunk. I hurried back up the stairs, threw open the basement door. Apart from a few small smudges, the floor was clean and unmarked—but in the middle of the grey speckled linoleum stood Maryan's large heavy chef's knife, wobbling slightly, its point plunged down into the floor. I felt a cool breeze against my ankle and saw that the back door that I had locked was now open, creaking softly, spilling golden streetlight into the room. I knew I should be frightened, but instead I was intrigued. Maryan had often warned of men who might come in the night and try to hurt me. Was that what this had been? I pulled the knife from the floor with a yank, held it out in front of me as I made my way to the back door, peering around and above me and then outside, then shut the door with a shove once again. Maryan always locked all three deadbolts.

I only ever bothered with the middle one, the oldest and probably the easiest to defeat. This time I turned them all with a defiant click-click-click.

"Lena?" Maryan called sleepily.

"Yes, Maryan, sorry," I answered. "Go back to sleep."

I put the knife in the sink, turned and looked down at where it had stabbed the floor. Knelt down, smoothed the scar with my fingers. *Trouble*, I whispered. Whenever a knife is dropped, trouble comes from wherever it points. And if the knife had been pointing down to the basement, that meant the trouble was coming from me, or to me, or from somewhere below me.

The next morning I came up the stairs into the kitchen to find Maryan sitting at the table, a mug of salted kelp tea already waiting for me. I sat down carefully, brought the steaming cup to my lips, took a still-too-hot sip. She saw the way I was holding myself and frowned. "Let me look."

I moved my chair to the centre of the room, stripped to my waist, crossed my arms on my chest and leaned forward, resting my chest against my thighs.

"Well now," Maryan said as she pulled another chair closer. "One of your sutures is loose." I could feel her as she ran her fingers along my spine, pressing and pushing my skin the way one would nudge and knead sweet yeast dough. "When did this happen? Do you remember?"

"Yesterday," I said, looking at her bare feet on the floor. Tiny toes, nails painted ruby red. "I was in the market, shopping. With a friend." I thought of the face sprayed on the wall, the postering guy, the hand at the small of my back. "I might have been carrying too much."

"You must be careful," she replied, getting up. She pulled one wooden drawer open, slid it shut, pulled open another, rummaged around with a clatter. Then came back to her chair, unzipped a small cloth case. I felt the sharp sting of alcohol as she swabbed the area above my buttocks. "Hold still," she warned—then began, so softly, to sing the song I'd known from childhood: the song that was sung not to me, but to that which lay coiled within me.

Malen'kiy sprut, malen'kiy sprut, ya tvoy drug . . . Malen'kiy sprut, malen'kiy sprut, ya pomogu. . . .

I turned my head and watched as she pulled a semi-circular needle out of the bag, then felt first one stitch come free, then another. I heard the snick of a small pair of scissors as she trimmed the end of the thread, then felt the curve of the needle as it pulled through one of the now-empty holes in my skin. I made a noise as she pulled it snug and then tied it to the stitch below. "There, that should hold," she said, sounding quite pleased. She pulled another length of waxed thread from the spool, snipped it, slipped it onto the needle and drew back and forth it through the remaining holes, criss-crossing the slit down my back like a shoelace.

"I do not think of you as having friends. How long have you known this friend?"

"Not long," I said, wincing.

As she began to tighten the thread, she gave a sudden gasp—and a droplet of blood splashed to the floor between our feet.

"Are you okay?" I asked.

"Yes, yes, I'm fine. Little teeth." I turned my head to see her sucking her finger.

"Is it back inside?"

"Yes," she answered, examining her finger, then wrapping it in a bit of tissue. "I startled it, I think. We are both very lucky." She took the two ends of the thread, gave a good tug, then tied them off. Both of us sighed, at that moment realizing we had scarcely dared to breathe. Two more snips to cut down the ends, a long strip of gauze secured with medical tape, and then she placed her hand on the nape of my neck.

"You can sit up now. Put on your blouse, and finish your tea." I fastened the buttons, knotted the silver-blue scarf I had worn, smoothed out my skirt. I drank down the tea, which by now had cooled, its saltiness more pronounced. She placed the scissors, thread and alcohol wipes back in the little cloth pouch, zipped it shut.

Later, I wondered if Maryan had been the intruder—if she had crept out of her bedroom while I was downstairs, had unlocked the back door, had dropped the knife and then hurried back to her bed.

Later still, I wondered if, instead, Alice had followed me home. *If you were a monster, what kind would you be?*

Saturday and Sunday were very long days at the

library, and long evenings thinking about Alice and her many questions. As I got close to the restaurant I wondered if she would stand me up. I had overheard two girls talking in the cafe about boys who had stood them up. One of them seemed intense and difficult and I decided that she and I were very alike. Of the many people I saw each day, very few of them noticed me, and those that did looked startled, even afraid of me.

So I came to the conclusion that Alice would stand me up, that I would wait patiently drinking green tea until it was clear to the server, the sushi master, the other patrons, that the person I was waiting for was never going to show. But when I swung open the restaurant door, Alice was already there and seated at a corner table. She stood and smiled and gave me a hug. I almost started to cry, I was so happy. And Little Sprout was still and silent.

"You have a secret," she said, in between bites of unagi roll. "I mean, we all have secrets, but you carry yourself in a particular way. Like there's something you don't want people to see about you."

I looked down at my plate, at the shrimp on its hard-packed bed of rice, shelled and flayed with just its pinkish tail remaining. "I have a kind of deformity, on my spine, a growth. Like a tumour. It's not painful, not usually, but it spasms from time to time and that's how I know I need to go home and rest. Bad things happen if I don't."

She looked shocked, as if she had imagined an

entirely different secret and now wasn't sure what to say.

"Like a tumour. Is it a tumour? Like cancer?"

"No," I replied, "not exactly. But it is wrapped around my spine, and it can't be removed. Not without killing me. That's what they say," I shrugged.

"Who are 'they'?" she asked. These were not the questions she was used to asking. These were uncomfortable questions, and she was uncomfortable asking them.

"The doctors. My aunt. Some specialists I used to go to. We don't talk about it much anymore." The trick to telling lies, I knew, was to make everything half-true. I picked up the shrimp roll with my chopsticks, dipped it in wasabi soy and then popped it in my mouth, pausing mid-chew to pull out the tail.

"Have you seen it? The growth?" I shook my head. "Not even in x-rays?"

"No," I answered. "I don't need to see it. I know it's there. I—talk to it, sometimes."

"Does it ever answer?" She ventured a smile.

I smiled back. "Not yet."

Alice nodded solemnly and then, all out of questions, she finished her unagi roll and poured out the last of the tea.

Dinner was largely silent after that. When we finished, I walked her back to her building. I was certain that this would be the end, the point where she would say "Well, it was nice knowing you," and pull my head down to give me a peck on the forehead. But instead, she wordlessly led me along her street, up to her building, into her lobby—*Wait, what was that handbill? Back there, on the fence—Was that a face?*—into her apartment and into her bedroom, then began to take off her clothes.

"I can't," I said quietly.

"You don't have to," she replied.

We lay down together on the bed, kissed and touched each other, her reaching into my blouse, into my pants. It all started out awkwardly, tinged with sadness, but then something between us turned and she rolled me on my back and straddled me, placed my fingers on her and inside her, and rode them until we both were wet and gasping. Another first. She collapsed on top of me, sweaty and giggly and swoony, then rolled off and landed beside me.

"Thanks," she said. "I needed that."

"You did most of the work."

"It was fifty-fifty. Or maybe sixty-forty." She turned towards me, leaned up on one elbow. "I know you don't want me to see, and that's okay, I totally get it. But I could just—touch it? Rest my hand on it?"

"I don't think that's a good idea," I sighed. What I wanted to say was: *I don't want it to know who you are.* Even at that moment, I could feel it was awake, awake and aware. Instead I said, "It's very sensitive, it's hard to even wear clothes sometimes."

"Then take them off," she said coyly. I shook my head, smiling.

"One day I will, but not today."

She put her arm around me, carefully, as if she

thought I might push her away. "I just want you to know that whatever you have, I'm good with it. Whatever it is, we have it together." This seemed like an impossible thing to say, but maybe that's how it works. Maybe that's when we can accept the most from each other, at the very beginning—before we can imagine what we have agreed to accept.

Alice fell asleep soon after, and soon after that I slipped out from beside her and made my way out of her apartment, out of her building. I found the fence, and the handbill pasted to it. On the handbill was a face, a woman's face, wreathed in fire or snakes or a wild mane of hair. Someone had tried to tear it off, the upper edge was ragged and rough. There had been some wording, you could see where some of the letters had been, but the words themselves were gone. Was this the same image that I saw in the graffiti? Whose face was it? And who was she to me?

Little Sprout twitched.

I glanced across the street and saw a man, two men, watching me. Standing apart, but somehow together. Little Sprout twitched again. I pulled my coat tighter around me and hurried home, keeping to the well-lit streets and surrounding myself with crowds.

The next morning, I came upstairs to find Maryan setting out a breakfast of boiled eggs and cucumbers and white cheese and brown bread. Out of nowhere, she asked: "Have you had any headaches or body aches? Fever or chills? Have you seen or felt anything unusual?"

Like what—the touch on my back, the image sprayed on the wall? A lithe young woman, naked, her body curled against mine? I shook my head no.

She picked up a heel of bread and smeared it with bacon drippings she kept in a bowl in the fridge. She had told me many stories about my mother at this table, over meals like this. I knew they couldn't have been true, but I loved hearing them regardless. One was that she had been a prima ballerina who had toured the world, another was that she had been a trapeze artist in the Bolshoi Circus, and in another she was a celebrated designer who had slipped through the Iron Curtain. But this time, Maryan told me a different kind of story, one I had never heard before.

"When my brothers and I were young, just ten or eleven, when we were still living in Krakow, your mother was brought to our family. She was only six years old. Her parents had been killed in a fire, we never learned by whom or why. She came to our door with two men and a woman—my parents knew them as the *vartivnyk*, the keepers. For five years, the keepers had moved from city to village to town, from country to country, and had come to ask my parents to take this girl, this child, across the ocean to the new land and then to hide her from sight. They would make the arrangements, pay for everything we needed, and help us settle wherever we wished. They bought this house for us. They paid us a monthly fee for our efforts. And so we made a new life for ourselves. And while we went to school and played with our friends, your mother stayed down in the basement. There was no apartment back then, just a bed in the corner with a few books and toys. We lived upstairs, as if she didn't exist. We were never to speak of her to anyone. I was the only one allowed to visit and play with her, to read to her, and even then never alone.

"As we grew older, I discovered that your mother would come up from the basement in the middle of the night, unlock the back door, and then vanish into the streets until just before dawn. She would then slip back in, relock the door, and go back down to her corner. Very early one morning I woke from my bed and went down to the kitchen to wait for her. She crept in like a cat, turned the bolt on the door, then saw me and froze. Right there in the doorway. She was covered almost head to toe with blood. Blood in her hair. Blood in her teeth. I knew the blood was not hers.

"We stared at each other for what seemed like hours, and then she walked past me and down into the basement, pulling the door shut behind her. My parents began to lock it at night, but that didn't matter. There was a wood-covered hole that had once been a coal chute—of course, that's long gone now. But that was what she used when she went out at night. I realized my parents were afraid of her even as we sheltered her, they were afraid that she would one day turn her hunger on us. But I was not afraid of her. I loved her. I should have been afraid."

Maryan looked up at me, looked back down at her plate. Took another piece of bread, dipped it in the grease.

"One morning, she brought you home, nearly naked, afraid—you were four, maybe five years old. I doubt you remember any of this." I shook my head. "My own father had died the year before, my brothers were away at a school. My mother and I were alone. Panicked out of her mind, she made a telephone call, and within a few hours the *vartivnyk* arrived—not the same keepers I saw in Krakow, but three others with the same dark clothes and severe expressions. I remember I was surprised to see them here, in the new land, but I now know that no matter how far or how fast we run, our ghosts and demons run with us, and are always close at hand. One of the keepers sat with us, a girl younger than me, while the two older men went downstairs. When they were finished, your mother had passed from this life. They had removed the *sprut* from her body and had placed it in yours. And my mother and I were left to care for you."

I was so shocked to hear this, I struggled to piece it together. "So she—was not my mother? She stole me? Where are my parents?"

"Your birth parents were killed," she said bluntly, "and when they were killed, she became your mother, if only for a moment. She brought you here so that you could live. And as she passed, she gave you a wondrous gift."

"A gift?" I was astonished. "It's a parasite. It's feeding on me, crippling me. I'm a murderer, thanks to this gift—and so was she!"

"I wish things could be different, but they are not. I have protected you as long as I could, and I have made difficult choices. It is time for you to know the truth. What you carry inside you is one thousand years old, and must live one thousand years more." She took the plates from the table, set them in the sink, then came over to me, and then kissed me on the top of my forehead. "Now," she said. "You must be watchful. Danger is around you, and inside you as well—held back by a thread, but not for long. I no longer know how to reach the keepers, but I know that they are watching. And so are those who would harm you. If nothing else, you must understand this: your time is coming soon."

I wanted to speak but no words would come. I shivered, felt a twitch and a quiver along my spine. Maryan took me by the hand, led me to the basement door, gently ushered me down the first step. "Be careful of your friend," she said. "And stay away from the market. It is not safe."

Another kiss, this time on my cheek. "Get some rest."

The twitch along my spine once more, and then a slipping down into stillness. I started down the stairs as Maryan closed the basement door, and for the first time I heard the click of the lock behind me.

I slept on and off all day and into the evening, and wondered if I was falling ill. I couldn't seem to get warm. As midnight came and went, I was still half in a daze after all that Maryan had said, and I decided to go back to see if I could find the first wall, the one where the graffiti had been postered over. Even if I couldn't scrape it clean, I might find something else, a clue. I couldn't guess why the image meant so much to me, but it did. I was compelled.

The market was in an old part of the city. Shops came and went here, houses were torn down and built back up, but you could have held a photo up from a hundred years ago and seen the same streets, the same churches, maybe even some of the same eyes and jawlines. I imagined the present slipping away with every step, the past rising up all around and taking hold.

I thudded to a halt at a stop light, looked up, and saw that I was a block or so away from where I thought the wall would be. Across the street, a delivery truck, tagged on one side with a jaunty scrawl, pulled away from the curb and sped by to catch the light, the driver leaning on the horn. As it whipped past, I saw the back of the truck had been sprayed with the same image, the same woman's face, that I'd seen earlier—neon green this time and obviously a stencil, slightly askew with overspray around the edges. As if realizing it had caught my eye, the truck abruptly turned a corner and flew out of sight.

But now I was curious: where else would I find it? Instead of continuing east to the wall, I began to walk south, casting my eyes across storefronts and newspaper boxes, peering down alleys, searching out any sign of another similar image. It was late now, and all around me the shops and cafes were starting to close. As I approached the end of the block, a greengrocer started to bring down the large steel shutter that covered his storefront. On it was the face, just a few feet away from me, this time sprayed in purple. The same woman's face, surrounded by—spikes? Shards? I stopped him, asked him, "Do you know what this is? How long has it been here?" He shook his head at me, shooed me away. "Closed! Closed!" I pointed at the face and he looked at it, disgusted—then ducked under the shutter and pulled it down with a slam. I took out my phone, snapped a shot of the image. I wondered if Maryan or Alice might recognize it—but some small voice, at once inside and outside, whispered: *No. Do not tell anyone.*

The next morning I felt better, so I messaged back and forth with Alice from the library and saw her between classes, at a Japanese spot near her campus. "Penny for your thoughts," she said as I sipped my cool green bubble tea. The tapioca beads were round and fat and black and I was determined to capture all of them with my oversized straw. I had been thinking of the sea witch, stabbed by the young girl rescuing her sailor brother. She had clutched her heart and fallen backward into the tide pool below, had floated out and expelled her cache of eggs into the ocean as she died. And then the embryos had bobbed aimlessly in the darkness of their shells, orphaned, alone, until they burst through into the water, the light, the new unknown. Some swallowed by fish, others scooped up by birds, until only a very few survived.

But instead of this, I looked down at the waves and swirls scoured into the steel countertop and said: "I'm worried about Maryan. She's imagining things now, spies and intruders and such." I frowned, stirring circles in the milky green liquid. "She barely goes out, sometimes she spends the whole day in bed. I'm afraid she'll hurt someone, or maybe herself. I would talk to a doctor, but she hasn't been to one for years."

"Isn't there someone you could call? Any brothers or sisters or cousins?"

"Two brothers, I think." I stirred and I stirred. "But I've never met them or spoken to them. I don't know where they are, or even their names."

"When my dad died, I found some stuff in a tin box in the garage, and then some other things in a safety deposit box. She might have some legal documents, a birth certificate, something about the house. At least it would be a start."

"I'm sorry about your dad," I said.

"It's okay, it was years ago."

"How did he die?"

"He was hit by a car," she replied. "Nothing special, and I guess that's the sad thing. People die every day."

A ping from her phone—a message, or an appointment alert. She glanced down at the screen and then jumped up suddenly. "Shit, sorry, I have to run. But let me know if you find anything." She leaned in towards me, gave me a quick kiss on the cheek, then turned and ran out the door, bells jingling in her wake.

It was just a few minutes later, when I was on my way home, when I saw the face once again. I had only walked four or five blocks when something caught my eye across the street, on a weathered wooden fence behind an old empty bank building, a shock of bright yellow.

I slowed and stopped and stared. It was the same image, the same face, that I had seen in the market. But what exactly was it? I waited for a break in the traffic, then sprinted across the street to look at it more closely. This one was clearer. And below it, a few words in Russian or Polish, or possibly Czech.

I took out my phone, snapped a few photos, then something—a dizziness, some kind of nausea—swept over me for a second, the pit of my stomach dropping, the way it does in an earthquake. I dropped the phone, crouched to pick it up and nearly fell over. I stood and leaned against the wall, next to the face, my hand touching it, and I waited for the world to right itself.

After a moment, I heard a car pull up with a small screech, the slam of a door. I looked up and saw a small dark-featured man standing over me, obviously worried. He was saying something about a hospital, emergency. I shook my head. It was like he was calling to me through a heavy grey fog. I mumbled Maryan's address. He nodded, reached down, lifted me by my arm, helped me into the back of his taxi, then hopped into the front and sped me away. I was dizzy and tired and thirsty. I wanted to sleep, my eyes were stinging. Every few blocks the driver would glance at me in the rear-view mirror. His expression told me to be afraid, but I was oddly calm.

I reached into my back pocket, pulled out my phone, thumbed through the photos I'd taken. This time, something about the face seemed familiar. A singer, perhaps, or an actress? ОНА БЛИЗКА. A name, a place? Maryan would know what it meant.

And then suddenly, the house, the yard, the door. I reached back to take out my wallet, then saw the meter was off. He shook his head—no pay, no pay—then asked if I needed help. No, I answered, and thanked him, pushed open the door and stood up, stood against it for a moment, then propelled myself to the gate. *I must look drunk*, I remember thinking, so I turned back and smiled weakly, waved him away. ОНА БЛИЗКА. I found my way to the side of the house, down the stairs to my door. Then the key, and the bolt, and the shoes, and the bed, and then blackness.

This was the dream, so real, so close: I felt a rhythmic rocking movement and a soft steady roar filled my ears, like the ocean in a seashell. I opened my eyes, and Alice was there, holding me. I was in the back of a car, lush and dark and soft, and the cab driver was there with me and Alice, he was speaking to someone—he was on a cellphone, speaking to someone in the old language, the one that I'd heard Maryan use. I wondered if Maryan was in the car as well, I must have said her name. Alice trembled, the cab driver looked at me, alarmed, and started speaking louder and faster.

Alice brought her lips to my ears and said, "Lena, your aunt is dead. Someone broke in and killed her. I followed you home, to see where you live—I know that I shouldn't have—but as I got closer I heard a scream, I saw these two men run out of your house, they looked—I don't know, like cops. This man next to you, he was in his cab waiting outside, he said you hadn't looked well. We went inside and found your aunt, and then we found you. He said he knew where to take you. Something's wrong, Lena, something's wrong with you and I'm so afraid."

I wanted to tell her that it was all right, that we would be fine, but I couldn't catch enough breath to speak and I was cold, I couldn't get warm and my teeth were chattering. She pulled me up against her, held me close, and her hand slipped down my back, down over Little Sprout, and I wanted to warn her but I couldn't speak, I couldn't breathe, and Little Sprout twisted and turned under her touch and she first pulled away, then placed her hand back over it and gently stroked it back and forth until it calmed.

The car veered off to the right and came to a sudden stop. The door swung open and the cab driver placed his arms around me, lifted me, swept me out of the back seat. I saw we were parked on the outskirts of the market, around the corner from the greengrocer. He carried me down an alley as Alice followed, gestured for Alice to take his keys and open an unmarked door, then led us through a small hallway and down a dark flight of stone stairs into what seemed like an old ruined church, a church beneath the streets. The face was here, the graffiti was here, overwhelming the wall at the front of the room. ОНА БЛИЗКА it said below the face, and beneath that it said SHE IS NEAR. And it was then that I realized: the face was me, the woman was me. I had been near, all this time. And now, here

I was.

Little Sprout stirred again and it was as if I shared its thoughts: its mother had been the true sea witch, the first of its kind, and now its new host would make the journey to its home in the northern waters, to assume its place and its power.

Dozens of people waited here, some of them old, but some younger as well. I knew these were the keepers, and with them we would be safe. *"Malen'kiy sprut, malen'kiy sprut, ya tvoy drug,"* they sang. *"Malen'kiy sprut, malen'kiy sprut, ya pomogu."*

"What are you doing?" an old woman asked. "She is starting to pass! We need a new host!"

"Let me see it," Alice said. The old woman shook her head.

"Where is Maryan?" another demanded. Others shouted out in agreement.

"Maryan walked away years ago," a much older man said loudly. "And now she is dead. We will not speak of her again."

"Let me see it," Alice repeated. "Please. I want to see it."

"Are you crazy?" a younger woman shouted. "We do not know who this person is!"

"We have no time!" the oldest man shouted back.

"Show her," I rasped. "Please, show her."

The oldest man nodded and the cab driver took me to the front of the room, placed me on my side on a long table, and I curled into myself as the oldest man lifted up my blouse, unfolded a small pocket knife and cut through the sutures one by one. I could feel him use the tip of the blade to peel back the skin along my spine. Alice reached forward. "No," he said. "You must not touch it." But then I felt Alice press her hand against me, against Little Sprout, caressing us, soothing us both.

"Yes," she said. "I can do this. Please." And then she climbed up onto the table facing me. I could see over her shoulder as another man took the pocket knife, pulled up the back of her shirt. She winced, eyes tearing, as he sliced into her.

"You don't have to," I whispered.

"I want to," she said.

I felt a tugging, a disentangling behind me, and then suddenly I was so tired, I could barely keep my eyes open. The oldest man stepped forward with something in his hands—the *malen'kiy sprut*, the "little sprout" that I had carried within me since I was a child, and that my not-mother had carried within her. It was not, in truth, an actual *sprut* but one of its distant cousins, a long thin gelatinous creature with one large bright eye, another smaller dark eye, and dozens of fine glassy tendrils studded with tiny shards of bone. Little teeth. The oldest man swiftly moved behind Alice, held the creature down behind her. She cried out, let out a half-dozen short sharp breaths, and then relaxed as he proceeded to stitch the wound and dress it.

I closed my eyes, and the darkness pressed against my face like a thick black curtain. And then light, and movement, red upon red upon red. I was somehow in two places—one cold and distant, the other warm and moist and close. I stretched and entwined and unfurled. I had a thousand fingers and I could touch and taste and think with all of them.

"Where am I?" I whispered. "Am I inside you?"

"Yes," she said softly. "You are."

"People die every day . . . isn't that right?"

"Yes," she said. "They do."

"Am I a monster?" I asked, with my old body's last breath.

"Yes," she sighed back. "A beautiful monster. And soon, the whole world will see."

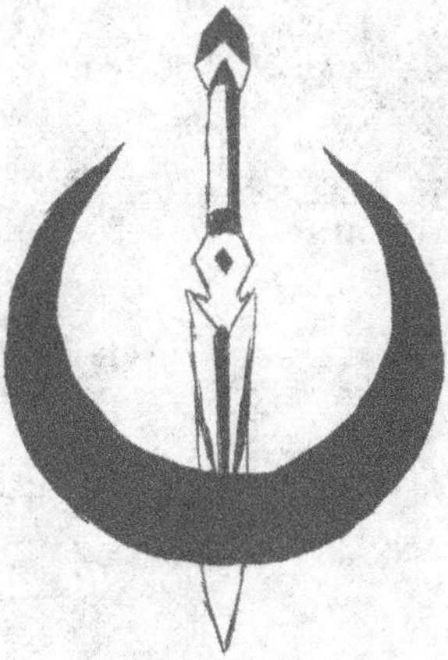

LIVIA

There are tales, where I come from, about a girl who walks. You may have heard them, you may have told them yourself. A girl, sometimes very young, sometimes older, fourteen or fifteen, sometimes sixteen, who walks along a lonely stretch of road. A road where something happened. Hundreds have seen her over the years. She never ages, never changes. At first you can't see her face. You think maybe she's lost, or hurt in some way. She stops, and when you approach her, she turns to look at you. And then she vanishes. So many stories, I am certain you've heard them.

Where I was born, there were once three small towns, and roads of course between them. The towns are gone, but the roads remain, including the road where the girl walks. Other roads in the area were improved years ago, covered with asphalt, painted with clean white lines, but not this road. The workers refused to work on this road.

The *oblast* administrators were outraged, said they would bring in new workers, from one of the cities, where desperate people would go anywhere and do anything for a few rubles. The workers said "Bring in whomever you like." They finished the other six roads on the list, even the ravine road that was long and twisted with sharp sudden turns, but they would not touch the short straight road where the girl, it was said, had died. Either the administrators had no success, or they didn't bother to try. No one was brought in from the city. No one did anything for any number of rubles. The road is what it was eighty years ago, a worn stretch of dirt with a hasty sprinkling of gravel. On some maps it doesn't even exist. People come upon it and wonder, "Where does that lead?" Then they feel a shiver for no clear reason, and go off in another direction.

The stories themselves of course are absurd. One is that the girl was deaf, was walking on the road alone, and did not hear the cart coming up from behind her, did not hear the shouts of the driver, who was young and not in control of his horses, and so she was trampled to death. A deaf girl would still have felt the rumble of the cart, would have smelled the dust in the air, would have turned around and jumped aside. Of this I am quite sure.

Another story is that the girl was walking with a young suitor after a dance or a wedding or some other occasion. He lived in one town, she in the other. He made jealous remarks about another young man who spoke to the girl or danced with the girl, and she said something or did something or said nothing at all, it's always the girl in these stories, and he lashed out and struck her and knocked her to the ground and she died. He may have struck her more than once. Other things, worse things, may have happened. The story depends not on the truth but the teller. What he leaves in, what he takes out. But still, dead. On the road or pushed into a ditch. This is an old story, you hear it everywhere. However, I can assure you, this girl had no suitor, not even in secret. These towns rarely had dances or weddings, and there is no ditch along that road. It is even and dry and edged on either side by farmers' fences and waving wild grasses.

And as always the beast story—they are so common here, in these parts. A girl walks along the road alone, quite late or quite early. She sees a shadow, low and long, lying on the ground ahead—a man, or an animal, possibly injured. She wants to help, hurries to help—it's always the girl in these stories—and then of course the shadow is a man, and the man is dead, horribly mauled, and the beast springs out from somewhere, all claws and teeth. Or the man is in fact the beast, if that can be said to be a fact, and it cannot. There was no beast, there was no shadow. Though if he was a beast, perhaps now she is one as well.

What there was, is this: a girl, a road, the late summer sun. The grasses are just starting to brown, the leaves on distant trees just lightly touched with red and gold. She has walked this road, between the towns, so many times since childhood, first with her father or mother, then with neighbouring friends, or alone, and she has always felt safe.

Today is different. The road is different, though of course it is the same road. It may be the heat, or the way the sunlight falls, the road seems very long today, strangely so. She stops and looks back and wonders if she has turned herself around somehow, if she is walking the wrong way, is somehow heading back from where she came. Neither town is in sight. There is only the road.

The girl has done nothing wrong. She is not injured, not in pain, not in any obvious danger. But somehow the road she is on is no longer the road she *was* on, she is somewhere else now. The road has no beginning, and now it has no end. The heat, the light, the late summer sun. And now this road can be any road, can be the road you walk along tonight. Your mind wanders as you walk and you find yourself by yourself, looking forward, looking back—you don't remember when the world fell away, but here you are. And ahead, the figure, the girl from all the stories. Perhaps she is lost, or confused in some way. She slows, she stops, and when you approach her, she turns to look at you. And then she is gone.

And this road, this is your road now. And you, now you are the girl, the story, and you are waiting to be told.